ALSO BY DAVID ROSENFELT

SANTA'S LITTLE YELPERS

ALSO BY DAVID ROSENFELT

SANTA'S LITTLE YELPERS

David Rosenfelt

MINOTAUR BOOKS
NEW YORK

First published in the United States by Minotaur Books, an imprint of St. Martin's Publishing Group

SANTA'S LITTLE YELPERS. Copyright © 2022 by Tara Productions Inc. All rights reserved. Printed in the United States of America. For information, address St. Martin's Publishing Group, 120 Broadway, New York, NY 10271.

www.minotaurbooks.com

Library of Congress Cataloging-in-Publication Data

Names: Rosenfelt, David, author.
Title: Santa's little yelpers / David Rosenfelt.
Description: First Edition. | New York : Minotaur Books, 2022. | Series: An Andy Carpenter novel ; 26
Identifiers: LCCN 2022027254 | ISBN 9781250828811 (hardcover) | ISBN 9781250828828 (ebook)
Subjects: LCGFT: Novels.
Classification: LCC PS3618.O838 S36 2022 | DDC 813/.6—dc23
LC record available at https://lccn.loc.gov/2022027254

Our books may be purchased in bulk for promotional, educational, or business use. Please contact your local bookseller or the Macmillan Corporate and Premium Sales Department at 1-800-221-7945, extension 5442, or by email at MacmillanSpecialMarkets@macmillan.com.

First Edition: 2022

10 9 8 7 6 5 4 3 2 1

In memory of Debbie Lynn Matoren,
the daughter of Gary M. Matoren

SANTA'S
LITTLE
YELPERS

It was your typical father-son evening, at least as typical as it can be when the father involved is a powerful mob boss.

Paul Donnelly Sr.'s base of criminal operations was in the Bronx, but his tentacles reached into other boroughs, as well as Westchester and Long Island. The kind of activities that he was involved in had little respect for borders.

Paul Donnelly Jr. always had a rather complicated relationship with his father. He never wanted anything to do with the family business, and Paul Sr. had over time developed mixed feelings about that. While he wanted Paul Jr. to respect him and follow in his footsteps, he also took a real measure of pride in what his son had achieved, mostly on his own.

For someone in Paul Sr.'s position, one of the basic goals is always survival. One mistake is too many. He had managed to endure and thrive quite successfully, but part of him was glad that his son did not have that burden.

Paul Jr. had carved out a place in the world of precious stones; he always loved and understood real beauty, whether it be art, opera, or jewelry. He was the first to admit that his father's money, however dishonorably earned, had helped greatly along the way. His father never understood or cared for the things that his son loved, but had come to respect his accomplishments.

On this night they did not discuss either of their businesses; they instead enjoyed a shared passion they had for harness racing. They went to Yonkers Raceway, sat in their private box, and stayed for six races. Afterward they went to a favorite restaurant, the one they always ate at after a night of racing, Spumoni's, on Central Park Avenue.

Other diners at Spumoni's had no idea who Paul Sr. was, unless they noticed the security around him. He had no real competition to speak of in his world; he had vanquished his main rivals a long time before. But he had not gotten to his preeminent position by being careless.

Survival was everything.

After dinner they went outside, and seconds later the world seemed to explode. A car went by and sprayed bullets from the rear driver's-side window. The police would determine later that the shots were errant because of the speed at which the car was moving.

Seven bullets were fired. Six were wild and missed everything, and the seventh entered the skull of Paul Jr., killing him instantly. Paul Sr. emerged unscathed, except for the nightmare of having to watch his only son die.

Paul Sr. vowed and eventually got his revenge, but he would never fully recover emotionally from the guilt and horror of that night.

But if his enemies thought he would be scared into backing off from the most important project of his life, they were dead wrong.

Theodore George Paraskevakos has my undying respect and gratitude. He was a great man, yet for all his genius and heroism, he remains basically unknown.

Let me explain why I feel so strongly about Mr. Paraskevakos, or as I call him, TGP.

I hate telephones. I'm not talking about smartphones; I'm fine with texting, and emailing, and finding out the weather and sports scores. I love being able to google an actor's name I forgot, or who won the 1949 World Series. All that is good, so perhaps I should be more specific.

I hate talking on the telephone.

Actually, I'm not a big fan of talking at all. To anyone. A select few people are exempt from this . . . my wife, Laurie, and my son, Ricky, come to mind. But the great thing about them is that we can be in a room without talking, and no one minds. The pregnant pauses can last almost as long as a real-life pregnancy, and none of us get annoyed or pissed off.

Silence is golden.

I also don't mind talking to my friends Vince Sanders and Pete Stanton when we hang out at Charlie's Sports Bar. But that's because our conversation consists mostly of insults, with some sports thrown in. Insult talking and sports talking are acceptable forms of discourse, when done in moderation and in person.

And that's one of the many things I love about dogs. The human, in this case me, completely controls the dialogue. That's not to say the dog can't respond and convey his or her feelings and opinions. But they use a wag of the tail, or a smile, or a head tilt, or a growl. Tara, my golden retriever, communicates better and is more eloquent than 90 percent of the people I know. She is the Winston Churchill of dogs.

I certainly dislike talking in my occasional forays into a courtroom, but as a sometimes defense attorney I'm forced into it. I hate writing briefs even more than talking, but that's sort of beside the point since I have another lawyer who does that for me.

But telephone talking is the worst because talking is the entire purpose of being on the phone in the first place. There's nothing else to do; you have this thing stuck next to your ear and mouth and you have to keep feeding it.

It's intrusive. Part of the reason that people live in homes with doors and locks on those doors is that they want privacy and peace. Phones destroy that serenity. Suddenly a bell starts ringing and there's an outsider in your home, and you're forced to greet them. And most of the time you're expected to chitchat before they come to the point.

And sometimes there is no point! Chitchatting is an end in itself!

I hate Alexander Graham Bell for what he did, and that brings me to the aforementioned Theodore George Paraskevakos. TGP invented caller ID and, by doing so, provided a peephole on the telephone door through which one can look and choose to admit or ban the person calling.

I, Andy Carpenter, am probably the only person in America who is relieved to learn that an incoming call is from a telemarketer. At least they have a specific reason for calling; they're not looking to make small talk. And I'm quite sure they don't get offended if someone hangs up on them or screens their calls; they expect it. It's part of the job description.

Bottom line is that I am not antisocial, but I do have a definite bias against telephone conversation.

Of course there are exceptions, and I just had one. I called Chris Myers, who is a friend and technically an employee at the Tara Foundation. That's the dog rescue operation that my friend and former client Willie Miller and I run, along with Willie's wife, Sondra.

Chris answered and we dispensed with the "How are you?" in a few seconds. We both answered, "Good," since that's the only proper response. Except for maybe "Do I look fat in this dress?" and "Do you want a bite of my cake?," there is no question to which an honest answer is less welcome than "How are you?"

"We've got a problem with the puppies."

He answered, "I know. I assume you want me to solve it?"

"How'd you guess?" I asked if he had time to meet me down at the Foundation now.

"Sure. There's something I want to talk to you about as well."

Then we both hung up.

That was it.

first met Chris Myers when he was in prison.

Usually when I go to a prison to see someone, I bring along a heavy dose of guilt, since I'm invariably visiting a client of mine who got convicted despite my efforts. But Chris was never my client, so I was off the hook for that one.

I didn't know much about his case and still don't. I am aware that he was serving a two-year sentence for involuntary manslaughter, as the result of punching someone in a bar fight almost three years ago, resulting in the person's death. I'd heard that Chris could have gotten a lesser sentence if he copped a plea, but he insisted he was innocent, went to trial, and lost.

My meeting him in prison had nothing to do with his crime or his trial. Chris is a dog lover, and he used his time in the prison to start a program where inmates learned how to train rescue dogs who had not yet found their permanent homes, mostly because of behavioral issues.

It was a win-win for the dogs and for the inmates, and the program has continued and prospered since Chris got out. He had almost ten months shaved off his two-year sentence for good behavior, and because the prison was overcrowded. Since I like and respect him, I vouched for him to the parole board. The warden has let Chris continue in the program since his release, in a supervisory and consulting role.

Chris is, or I should say *was,* a lawyer. He worked in the litigation department for a Manhattan-based firm, but was disbarred once he was convicted of a felony. I would also love to be an ex-lawyer, sooner rather than later, but I'm not going to assault anyone to make it happen. I would be too afraid that the person I'd assault might return the favor.

Chris is already at the Foundation when I arrive, talking to Willie and Sondra. Willie and Sondra run the place day-to-day, and I help out when I can. When I'm not working on a case, which is my favorite time, I am able to do more.

Chris works here three days a week, not for the money, but because he enjoys it. Chris did well as a lawyer, and I believe he comes from some significant family money, so he's basically doing it because he loves dogs.

Lovable dogs are something we have in great supply.

Right now they are in greater supply than usual. A very pregnant golden retriever showed up at the Animal Shelter in Paterson about three weeks ago. Her tag identified her as Killian, but there was no address or owner information. My guess is the idiot owners did not want to deal with a pregnant dog, so they left her at the Animal Shelter, which means the morons left her to an uncertain fate.

We put up the obligatory signs and advertised online, knowing no owner would show up to claim her. When that proved to be the case, we took her. She is a fantastic dog and has had eight adorable puppies while in our care. She's patiently been nursing them ever since. But we're not set up to care for a litter of puppies; we generally rescue adult dogs.

The other problem is that with Christmas approaching, people will see cute puppies and want to give them as gifts. Giving a dog as a gift is generally a terrible idea; anyone who wants to adopt a dog should take the initiative on their own.

"I'll take care of the whole family at my house," Chris says. "My neighbor will help, she's always talking about how much she loves dogs, but her husband is allergic so she can't get one of her own."

Willie says, "Great. Sondra and I will take them in the van and follow you home. Thanks for doing this, my man."

"No problem. How long do you think it will be?"

"I'd say we can start placing them in about six weeks," Sondra says, and Chris and Willie both nod their approval.

While Willie and Sondra start getting Killian and her kids ready for the short trip, Chris asks if he can talk to me privately. Since only a couple of dogs are with us at the moment, I ask, "Can they listen in?"

He smiles. "Sure. I'm just a little paranoid."

"What's going on?"

"I think I can get my conviction overturned."

"How?"

"I've just learned that a witness lied. The main witness against me."

"How do you know this?" I'm not liking the sound of this; I hope that this is not an obsession for Chris that he is chasing with little chance of success.

"He told me he did. He said it's haunted him since then."

That changes the dynamic considerably. "He sought you out to say this, or you found him?"

"He came to me. I don't look back, Andy. I have been thinking I would have to accept the situation and move on, but I did not commit that crime, and if I can prove it, I would like that very much. I could also get my law license back. I didn't realize how much it would mean to me until the possibility came up."

"What's his name?"

"The witness? Charlie Burgess. He lives in Totowa, used to work at the post office. Although I think he might be retired."

"Did he say why he lied?"

"He told me he was paid to lie, but wouldn't say who paid him. He's afraid they will find out what he's doing."

It's time to address the legal elephant in the room. "How can I help?"

"You know your way around the criminal justice system, so I was hoping you can guide me through this. I'd pay you, of course."

I shake my head. "First of all, paying is not an option. Working at the Tara Foundation comes with low salary, no health benefits, but full legal services in the area of lying witnesses. Who was your lawyer on the original case?"

"Ronald Hoffman. He's retired, which is just as well. It's fair to say I was not thrilled with his representation, although the case against me was pretty strong. Total bullshit, but strong."

"Okay, so you want me to represent you in this?" I know the answer all too well.

"I do. I'm sorry. . . . I know how you feel about taking on clients, but this will hopefully be quick and painless. You'll have this wrapped up by Christmas."

It's never quick and painless is what I'm thinking and don't say. And since we just finished with Thanksgiving, there is no way a court will deal with this before Christmas. But I don't say that either.

What I say is "Happy to do it."

think you're doing a really nice thing," Laurie says, while we're having dinner.

"What are you doing, Dad?" Ricky asks.

"I'm helping someone with a work thing."

"Dad has a client," Laurie says.

"It sounds awful when you put it that way," I say, since I have for years now tried to avoid taking on clients, with unfortunately little success.

"It's your dad's friend Chris."

Ricky knows Chris and likes him a lot. "Great," he says, but then seems to lose interest.

"He seems to think it will be quick and painless," I say to Laurie.

"And it won't?"

"I haven't looked into it yet, so I don't know how painless it will be. But overturning a conviction is never quick; the system does not like to admit mistakes."

"When are you going to look into it?"

"Unfortunately, right after we finish dinner, so please keep the dessert and coffee coming; I want to put it off as long as I can. I have a transcript of the trial, and Chris wrote up all of his dealings with the witness. I was hoping to watch the Knicks game, but that's not going to happen."

"They're going to lose anyway." Laurie doesn't follow basketball, but I've told her enough about the Knicks over the years for her to be confident in her prediction.

I have so much coffee that I'm sloshing when I move, but eventually I have to recognize that dinner is over and it's time to go through the materials. Chris had requested a trial transcript through his lawyer soon after the trial; as a lawyer himself he wanted to examine it to see if he could find reason to appeal.

He didn't find anything and served his time, but it's why he had the transcript available to give to me.

As trial transcripts go, at least in my case experience, this is short. The entire trial lasted three days; the prosecution called six witnesses, and Chris's attorney called three. Chris's witnesses were character witnesses; they had no knowledge of the underlying facts. They were there simply to say that the Chris they knew could not have done such a thing. One of those witnesses was Chris's ex-wife, Jessica. Their marriage had broken up not long before that, but she was still there to support and vouch for him.

The jury took four hours to decide that the Chris they knew could do such a thing, and they came back with the guilty verdict. I'm surprised it took that long. If I were on the jury, I would also have voted to convict.

I'm not impressed with the job that Chris's attorney, Ronald Hoffman, did. While the facts were not in Chris's favor, Hoffman did a mediocre job cross-examining the prosecution witnesses. He seems to have been going through the motions; I can feel the lack of energy while reading these pages.

Without question, the key witness . . . and the reason Chris went to prison . . . was Charlie Burgess. He testified that he was there, in the alley behind the bar, when the fight started. He said Chris threw the first punch, and the victim, Joey Bonaventura, went down. Burgess described how he heard the thud when Bonaventura's head hit the pavement.

Hoffman couldn't touch Burgess on cross-examination. He said that he saw what he saw, and Hoffman was never able to find a reason why Burgess might have lied. In the face of that, the jury had no choice but to convict.

One thing I hadn't known, but which was covered extensively in the trial, is that Chris was an alcoholic. He was very drunk the night of the incident. I certainly have not seen any sign of that in the Chris that I have spent time with.

Once I finish with the transcript, I turn to the pages Chris gave me describing his recent interactions with Burgess. He says that Burgess contacted him, asking to meet in a location where they would not be seen.

That struck Chris as strange, but he agreed to the meeting. Once they were together, Burgess told him that he lied in his testimony, and it has haunted him ever since.

Burgess said he was paid to lie. He wouldn't say by whom, but Chris got the impression that Burgess was afraid of whoever it was.

Burgess said he was willing to testify in secret, once under oath, and was then planning to leave town. Chris could not say anything about it to anyone but the court, under a guarantee of confidentiality. Burgess would not talk to anyone else besides Chris and the authorities.

Any violation of this, and Burgess would deny everything. He was quite emphatic about that.

Mercifully, this limits what my role can be. For example, I will not be attempting to contact Burgess and discuss his testimony. Chris will be his contact. My function will simply be to go to the court and present our motion for a reversal of the conviction, and to arrange for Burgess's deposition under oath.

Chris thinks we have to get a reversal, which is difficult to do. In reality it's not our only option. If we get a new trial based on Burgess's recanting, Chris would prevail in that trial because the main witness, Burgess, would not testify for the prosecution.

So our first choice by far is to get the judge to overturn the original conviction, and the prosecution to accept it and not retry. I would describe it as a long shot, even with Burgess recanting. While we would win a new trial without Burgess, I can't imagine that Chris would want to sit through one, after having already served his time.

It is extremely unlikely that even a loss in a new trial would result in additional jail time. A US Supreme Court case, *North Carolina v. Pearce,* has virtually ruled that out as being "vindictive."

But for now, even though this case may not move quickly, I won't have that much to do. I'll have to set it all up with the court, then basically move out of the way.

I take a break to tuck Ricky into bed. He's rapidly getting too old for this; he's probably been too old for a while. I think he knows how much I enjoy it, so he lets me continue the tradition.

"Hey, Dad, some of the kids at school like Batman better than Superman."

"That's ridiculous. Superman all the way. Batman is just a guy with cool stuff; Superman is the one with the power."

Ricky nods. "Yeah, me too. Not even close."

Ricky has been into the superheroes, especially Superman, and we've been watching some of the films together. We've even found the old *Superman* TV shows with George Reeves on YouTube and watched some of them.

"At your age I was a big Superman fan; especially the whole X-ray vision thing," I say. "He could look through stuff or burn stuff, just with his eyes. I always was afraid he would make a mistake and burn stuff instead of looking through it."

Ricky laughs, and that continues to be the best sound I have ever heard in my life. "I like the way he can crush stuff in his hands, and, of course, the flying."

"Yup. If Batman ever tried to fly, he'd fall on his ass."

Another laugh out of Ricky, a kiss on his forehead, and I'm heading back to the den.

I call Eddie Dowd, who works with me in the firm, and I explain the situation to him. Eddie is much better at writing briefs than I am, and he actually likes doing it. So I ask him to prepare a motion with the supporting information, which we will present to the court.

"Sorry to dump this on you," I say, "but I'd like to get it in fast and put it behind us."

"No problem. It's a slam dunk."

Eddie is a former New York Giants football player from

back in the days when they were good, and he often talks in sports jargon.

I get off the phone, satisfied that we are moving as aggressively as we can. The speed at which this happens will be up to the justice system, which is to say it will move slowly.

It's the nature of the legal beast.

To what do I owe this visit?" Richard Wallace asks. "Are you dipping your toes back into the legal water?"

"What are you talking about?"

"You told me you were retiring."

"Yeah, and since I made that momentous announcement, I've had one client after another. I've since retracted it, so that every time I take a case I don't consider myself a retirement failure."

Richard laughs. For a while now he has been the chief prosecutor of Passaic County, a job my father once held. Dad was a mentor to Richard, who has long described him as a second father. Richard is one of the good guys.

"Okay, I stand corrected," he says. "So what are you doing here?"

"We just filed a motion with the court. It's confidential, but it will be making its way to your department, so I wanted to give you a heads-up. I'd like to move it along quickly, if possible."

"What is it?"

"Does the name Chris Myers mean anything to you?"

"I don't think so. I . . . is that the lawyer who killed a guy behind a bar?"

"You've got the right guy, but he didn't kill anyone."

"But he was convicted, right?"

"He was, wrongfully."

Richard smiles. "Don't you hate when that happens?"

"We're getting off track. The key witness against him is recanting and admitting that he was paid to lie."

Richard's face reflects his sudden interest. "Paid by who?"

"I don't know yet. But he will swear as to what really happened and didn't happen. Based on that, we are petitioning the court to reverse the conviction. Chris has already served his time, so that's not an issue, but I want it expunged from his record."

"No retrial?"

"That's a last resort. You'll see why when you read the brief. The witness is scared of something, most likely the people that paid him off."

"You've talked to the witness?" I'm hearing some skepticism in Richard's voice; at heart he is all prosecutor, as he should be.

"I have not. But I trust Chris completely, and either way it doesn't matter. The witness will either tell what he knows, or he won't. I'm just trying to set the process up and hopefully expedite it."

Richard nods. "Okay, I'll look at it personally. Obviously I can't make any promises."

"Understood."

We spend the next half hour reminiscing about my father. "When I have a decision to make, I still find myself trying to figure out what he would do," Richard says.

"Me too. His only flaw was that he was a Yankee fan.

But over time I have learned to forgive; we Met fans are big that way."

"I'm also a Yankee fan."

I shake my head. "Have you no moral compass?"

I leave Richard and call Chris on the way home. "How are the puppies doing?"

"They're a handful, but adorable."

"Thanks for doing this. I just called to tell you that we filed the brief with the court, and I've spoken to the prosecution about moving quickly. That's all we can do right now."

"Thanks, Andy."

"These things take time."

"I know. I used to be a lawyer and hopefully will be one again."

I don't bother mentioning that the reverse is true for me: I am a lawyer and hope not to be one soon. Instead I just say, "Let's try to make it happen."

It's starting to snow when I take Tara, Sebastian, and Hunter for our evening walk.

I like snow in theory. It looks beautiful when it's coming down, especially when set against the backdrop of houses strung with colorful Christmas lights. I still remember the thrill I got as a kid watching it snow and hoping it meant that school would be called off. It didn't happen much, but when it did . . . that was as good as it got.

The dogs love the snow, especially Tara. I've never met a golden retriever who didn't, but Tara has a special affinity for it. When it starts, she goes outside in the yard, lies down until she is covered, then shakes it off and starts all over again.

Hunter, our pug, likes anything Tara likes; she is his hero. Even Sebastian, our lazy basset hound, who has the energy level and dexterity of your average houseplant, seems to like it. He always waits until it stops, then goes outside and moves the snow around until it makes a comfortable bed. Everything represents a potential bed for Sebastian.

I'm looking forward to getting home from the walk because I've got a surprise for Ricky and Laurie. I can never think of a good Christmas present to get them, but I think I've come up with a gem this year.

This morning I booked a trip to Disney World; the plan is to spend a week there over Christmas vacation. It might be a long week for me, even though the woman at Disney that I booked it with said we would have a "magical experience." My goal, a modest one, is to watch Ricky have a great time.

I'm going to tell Laurie about it first, just in case she knows a reason we can't go. I don't want to tell Ricky, get him excited, and then have the whole thing blow up.

So I try to speed the walk along, but Sebastian is resistant to speed. It's also getting a bit slippery from the snow, so every one of his steps seems to take twenty minutes.

Ricky's not home; he's sleeping over at his friend Will Rubenstein's. That's fine, because I want to clear it with Laurie anyway. "I've got to give you your Christmas present now," I say.

"Andy . . ." With just that one word, and the tone with which she says it, Laurie is telling me her often-repeated belief that Christmas presents should be received and opened on Christmas morning. Laurie can substitute the word *Andy* for entire paragraphs; I don't know how she does it.

"I know, I know . . . but this time you have to make an exception. Because if you wait until Christmas morning, we'll have missed our flight."

"What kind of flight? Where are we going?"

"Disney World. I've been told we're going to have a magical experience."

"What a great idea. Ricky will go crazy."

We tried to do a trip like this a couple of years ago, but I wound up on a case that prevented us from going. I've felt bad about it ever since.

"I can't wait to tell him," I say.

"Is there any chance that this thing with Chris can force you to be home?"

"Zero. Even if the court was going to move that fast, which it won't, they're closed that week."

We spend the rest of the night figuring out flights, and other things we can do while we're down there. I'm really glad that Laurie is so into this; I know for certain that Ricky will be.

"Merry Christmas," I say.

"Nicely done, Andy."

This has gone so well that for the moment I'm not even minding the incessant Christmas music that Laurie plays in the house from Halloween through February. The only thing that could intrude on this pleasantness does so: the irritating ring of the telephone cuts through the good cheer.

I look at the caller ID and it's Chris, so I'm obligated to answer it.

"There's a problem," he says. "I got a text from Burgess; he said it's off."

"Why?"

"I don't know, when I texted him back he didn't answer. I'm going to find him and talk to him."

"Okay. I'll have to pull the motion first thing in the morning. We can't go to the well more than once on this; if we file and he doesn't testify, we won't be able to go back if he changes his mind again."

"I understand. I'll keep you posted. I'm really pissed off about this."

I hang up, and Laurie asks, "What happened?"

I tell her, and she asks, "Is the trip off?"

"No chance."

"Let's not tell Ricky for a few days, just to be sure."

Eddie informs the court that we are withdrawing the brief, saying cryptically that there are some issues with the witness.

I call Richard Wallace and say, "Disregard everything we talked about in your office, except for the parts about my father and the Yankees."

"What happened?"

"Apparently the witness is having cold feet."

"Okay. It was nice seeing you. Come in anytime you have a witness who is planning to recant his decision to recant."

I feel bad about this since I know it is important to Chris. I'm pretty sure it's about far more than getting his law license back; this was a chance to restore his reputation and respect. It's a shame that it has to depend on someone so obviously unreliable, and probably corrupt, as Burgess.

I call Chris to tell him what I've done and to say that the motion can be refiled at any time. He doesn't answer the phone, which I prefer, and I leave the message on the machine. I also ask him to inform me immediately if there are any changes in the situation, meaning if Burgess changes his mind yet again.

If he does recant his recanting of his recanting, we're going to have to come up with a different strategy. We will have to get him under oath before we go to the court; we cannot take a chance on messing up again.

Ricky comes home from school, but we're not going to tell him about Disney World until after dinner. Laurie is planning to make some kind of ceremonial presentation out of it; she even shows me a ridiculous hat with mouse ears on it that she bought for him.

There was never a point in my life that I would have worn a hat like that, and I have no doubt that the son of Andy Carpenter will soundly reject it as well. But I'm not about to tell Laurie that; let Ricky do the dirty work.

"Nice hat" is what I say. "With ears. Hard to find a good ear hat like that these days."

Ricky comes home and it's all I can do not to tell him, but Laurie and I agreed we'd wait until after dinner. "I'm hungry," I say. "Dinner almost ready?"

"It's three o'clock, Andy."

"Not in London." Then, "What time is it in Orlando?"

"Andy . . ." This time the word *Andy* can be interpreted as "You'd better shut up or you're going to be wearing a hat with ears."

So I decide to shut up.

Dinner starts and I can't wait for it to end so we can tell Ricky the surprise. But I have to be patient; it's harder to rush things at home. For instance, I can't ask for a check or tell the waiter to wrap up the food and we'll take it home.

We're just finishing up when the phone rings.

Laurie answers it and after a moment says, "We're eating

dinner, Pete. Can he call you back?" Then, "Okay, here he is." Laurie walks toward me with the phone. "Pete says it's important."

I could have told her that already, since Pete shares my aversion to telephone talking. He wouldn't be calling unless he had something significant to tell me.

Pete is the captain in charge of Homicide for the Paterson Police Department, as well as one of my Charlie's Sports Bar buddies.

"What's up, Pete?"

"Just giving you a heads-up. You're going to be receiving a call about Chris Myers." Pete also knows Chris and likes him.

"Is anything wrong? Is he okay?"

"He's okay, but there's plenty wrong."

"What happened?"

"Andy, he killed a guy. Again. But this time he meant to."

Chris calls me from the jail less than a minute after I get off the phone with Pete.

I've barely had time to start telling Laurie what is going on.

The caller ID says *Passaic County,* so I'm sure he is calling from the jail. "Andy, I've been arrested. They're accusing me of killing Charlie Burgess."

"Shit," I say, because I am at my most eloquent in situations like this.

"Yeah, he was shot to death."

My first thought is wondering how Chris would know how Burgess was killed; there is no chance the police would have shared that with him. When they make an arrest, they are in listening mode, not talking.

"Don't say another word." I don't want him saying anything incriminating on the jail phone, which can best be described as a party line.

"I understand."

"I'm coming down there now. Not one word to anyone."

Laurie has heard my end of the conversation, which has told her all she needs to know. But I fill her in on the few details she would have missed, like that Charlie Burgess is the victim.

"That's the guy who was going to recant his testimony?"

I nod. "The very one."

"This is not good."

I nod again. "I'm aware."

"We'll do the presentation to Ricky tomorrow."

"Laurie . . ."

"I've already figured it out. We'll just tell him we're going during spring vacation."

"I'm sorry about this." I am. But I can't argue the point because I know that once I get into a murder case, I will not have time to spend a week with people who wear ear hats.

"Not your fault. You're a lawyer; go do some lawyering."

"I made two mistakes in my life; how long do I have to pay for them?"

"What were the mistakes?"

"Law school was one. But I could have overcome that if I hadn't studied for the bar. That did me in."

She smiles. "We'll have our magical experience in the spring."

"What about the ear hat?"

"It will still be appropriate. It's timeless. Now get out of here and go see your client."

She's right; I have to go talk to Chris. He sure as hell can't come talk to me . . . there are bars and armed guards in the way.

Visiting a client in the county jail is either better or worse than visiting one in state prison, depending on your perspective. In jail the client has usually just been arrested, so he is stunned and scared. It's tough to see, especially since it's almost always certain that getting him his freedom will take a long time, if it happens at all. But at least the client is not yet reconciled to this being a permanent situation; he or she has some hope that some mistake has been made, or something might occur to prove his innocence.

State prison is far more depressing. The inmate is rarely hopeful; he has usually come to terms with his predicament. It's not even a predicament anymore; it's just a fact of life. That's also tough for me to see, especially since if I had done a better job at trial, he might not be there.

So while the person in jail might be hoping and expecting me to do something positive and immediate, the prison inmate knows better. That takes some of the pressure off.

This is not Chris's first time behind bars, so he doesn't have the look of panic I see so often.

"Thanks for coming down so fast, Andy," he says once we are sitting in the lawyer meeting room. He's in handcuffs, and a guard waits outside the door.

"Tell me everything you know about the situation."

"Okay. I told you I got a text from Burgess saying he was backing out, that he wouldn't testify. I responded, but he never answered. I kept trying but got nothing, so this afternoon I went to his house."

"Where?"

"In Totowa. I got there about five o'clock. I rang the bell but no one came to the door. I knew someone was home because I heard the television, and there were some lights on. So I pounded on the door. . . . I was really pissed."

"What happened then?"

"He wouldn't answer; he was obviously afraid to face me. But I was not letting him off the hook. The door was locked, so I went around toward the back and saw a window that was slightly open on the ground floor. I opened it and went through it, into the house."

I don't like where this is going, but I can do nothing but wait until he gets there.

"Sure enough, Burgess was there in the den. I scared the shit out of him when he saw me; this was a guy under a lot of stress. He was packing."

"Where was he going?"

"I don't know. I asked him and he said, 'Where no one can find me.'"

"I yelled at him, something like 'You can't bail out on me like this.' He yelled back that I should leave him alone, that I had no idea who he was dealing with."

"What else did he say?"

"Nothing. A few seconds later there was a gunshot, and he was thrown back against the wall. He was hit in the side of the head; it almost took his head off. Sprayed blood everywhere. I don't know where the bullet came from."

"There was no one in the house?"

"Not that I saw, but obviously someone was there, or maybe it came through a window. I don't know. I hit the ground once I realized what happened."

"Then what?"

"I panicked and ran. First of all, I was afraid of getting shot myself. But I also was afraid that if I was on the scene, I'd be blamed for it."

"Did you go back out through the window?"

"No. Through the front door. I think I left it open when

I ran, but I'm not sure. I drove home, and about three hours later the cops came and arrested me."

"You didn't tell them what you're telling me?"

"I didn't say anything to them."

"Good. I'm sure you know the drill. You'll be arraigned and bound over for trial. Bail is extremely unlikely, but we'll make the effort. Is there anything you need right now?"

"No. And don't worry, the puppies are okay."

"We'll get them."

"They're fine for the moment; my neighbor saw what was happening and she said she'd watch them tonight."

"Okay . . . good. We'll arrange to pick them up in the morning. I'll be back to talk to you soon, and I'll see you at the arraignment."

"Thanks, Andy. I know this is the last thing you want."

"No, the last thing I want is for you to be convicted of something you didn't do."

wish I could say for sure that Chris did not commit this crime.

I like him, which is not exactly a compelling defense to present to a jury, or even to myself. I have had guilty clients who I liked, but who were driven by circumstances to do something very wrong.

For all I know Chris possesses an inner, uncontrollable rage, which may now have caused him to snap twice. That he says he did not murder Burgess is not exactly proof or even particularly significant; guilty people professing innocence is not an entirely new concept.

I tend to follow my gut, although my gut is no better at predicting this stuff than I am at picking football winners. I can't remember the last start of an NFL season when I didn't think—bizarrely—the Giants would win the Super Bowl.

In this case, my gut believes Chris . . . sort of.

We obviously haven't gotten discovery yet, but police don't make an arrest within hours after a crime is committed unless they feel they have a good reason. They know that in Defense 101 lawyers are taught to claim that the cops and prosecutors rushed to judgment and thereby let the real criminal go free.

They were obviously not worried about that here, so they must have what they feel is evidence at a level beyond probable cause . . . heading toward proof beyond a reasonable doubt.

Maybe they're right . . . and maybe they're wrong. Criminal defense attorneys live in the world of "maybe they're wrong."

The arraignment is tomorrow, and there isn't much for us to do before then. I call Eddie Dowd and ask him to request discovery material immediately and also to find out who the lead counsel will be for the government. It doesn't matter that much; they're all pretty competent. Richard Wallace does not hire any stiffs.

I've called a meeting of our team. One reason is just to talk strategy in a nonspecific way; we'll get more into the weeds when we learn about the prosecution's case. The other, at this point more important reason, is to alert everyone that we are about to go to work, and that we have to hit the ground running.

Cases and investigations are most fruitful in the early days after the crime, before witnesses' stories and the attitude of the public get set in stone. So we will want to move quickly.

We're meeting at my house today. It's easier than my office, for a couple of reasons. For one, Laurie and I already live here. For another, my office is a bit of a dump. It's above a fruit stand on Van Houten Street in downtown Paterson, and when we stuff the whole team into my conference room, it barely leaves enough room for a ripe cantaloupe.

We meet in my den. People like to arrive fairly late for

these meetings, waiting until right at the time it's called for. That's because they want to let Marcus Clark arrive first, so they can choose a seat that's not next to him.

Marcus is a member of what's called the K Team; it's an investigative operation that also includes my wife, Laurie, and Corey Douglas. Both Laurie and Corey are ex-cops of the Paterson PD. The members are all competent investigators, but Marcus is also remarkably scary and dangerous.

Marcus is on our side, and he's a tremendous asset to us. But that doesn't mean anyone wants to sit near him. The problem is that if someone arrives too late, then the seat next to Marcus is the only one left. So obviously the situation is tricky and requires some serious strategizing.

Sam Willis got here last, so he drew the short straw and is sitting on a couch next to Marcus. Sam is my accountant in his other life, but for us he serves as a computer hacker. Sam has total access to everything in the cyber world, legal and illegal, and absolutely everything is in the cyber world.

The other member of the K Team is Simon Garfunkel, a German shepherd who was Corey's partner on the police force. Simon can't sing at all and has absolutely no interest in parsley, sage, rosemary, or thyme. He's a biscuit guy. But he is an excellent partner to have on our side if we need a bridge over troubled water.

Right now Simon is in the kitchen, playing with Tara and Hunter. I'm sure Sebastian is sleeping this one out.

Eddie Dowd, the other lawyer in the firm, sits with a notepad in front of him, ready to write down any pearls of wisdom that accidentally spill out of my mouth.

Notably without a notepad is Edna, my administrative

assistant, who has nothing to do with administration and hasn't assisted me in years. She is work-averse, and while that has always been the case, the condition has been exacerbated in recent months by her seemingly endless engagement.

Never married and in her sixties, Edna has found her guy, David Divine. She and David have been planning their nuptials 24–7, mostly traveling to potential locations for a destination wedding. My plan is to wait to come up with an excuse not to attend until a date and location are chosen.

In the meantime, I've been strategizing potential excuses. If it's in the Caribbean, it could trigger my latent piña colada allergy. If it's Europe, I'm thinking expired passport, though that's a little weak. If it's Disneyland, I'll probably have to go, but I'm not wearing the ear hat.

I'm sure Edna is crushed that we have a client, but in the short term she's probably relieved that the meeting is at the house. We don't have a Xerox machine here, so she can rest assured that she won't be stuck with the arduous task of copying anything.

Willie Miller sometimes comes to these meetings, and as a dangerous guy, he can usually help Marcus, Corey, and Laurie with the heavy lifting. But today he and Sondra are picking up Killian and the puppies from Chris's neighbor, so he couldn't make it.

There has not been that much publicity regarding the Burgess killing, so I'm not sure if everyone knows who our client is. Certainly Eddie does, because he filed the original brief, and obviously Laurie does as well.

I stand and turn to Laurie. "Before we start . . . any

chance we can turn off the Christmas music? 'Jingle Bells' doesn't seem to fit the occasion."

Laurie gives me a dirty look, but gets up and turns off the stereo system.

"We have a client." I pause for Edna to shudder. "It's Chris Myers. Some of you know him. He's a former lawyer who served time for involuntary manslaughter and now is accused of killing a man named Charlie Burgess.

"Burgess was the main witness against him in the manslaughter trial, and according to our client, he was set to recant that testimony. He then changed his mind, again according to Chris, and Chris went to his house to convince him to reconsider. While he was there, Burgess was shot by an unknown assailant. Chris panicked and ran and was arrested three hours later. You now know as much about this as I do."

"Did they find the murder weapon?" Corey asks.

"I don't know; we haven't gotten discovery yet."

"We will start receiving it tomorrow," Eddie says. "And by the way, Daniel Morrow is the lead prosecutor on it. He's new to the department; I don't think they see this as a tough case. My contacts in the office say that they think we'll plead it out."

"Is that possible?" Edna asks, forever hopeful.

"Remains to be seen." I very much doubt that Chris will plead it out, but I don't have the heart to crush Edna's spirit. "For us to prevail, this is going to have to be a much more complicated case than it appears on the surface. If Chris is innocent, and we have to operate as if that is a fact, then a whole boatload of questions have to be answered."

"Like what?" Laurie asks.

"Like why did Burgess lie in the earlier case? Like who was so afraid that he would recant that they permanently silenced him now? Like why would Chris have been framed twice; who was he a danger to? And why was he dangerous? Like who was the victim in the first case and was he significant to the overall picture, or just in the wrong place at the wrong time?

"If Chris is right, someone has gone to great pains to get rid of him. There has to be a reason for that, and there's an excellent chance that if we find out that reason, we will have found out everything.

"Sam, there will be a lot of research for you to do, as soon as we get the details. But for now, see what you can learn about the victim, Charlie Burgess. I know from the transcript he has done some time."

"I'm on it. And if you want me in the field, I can do that."

Sam wants to be a real detective, out on the street, shooting bad guys if possible. "Thanks, Sam, we'll keep that in mind. Stay ready."

I turn and address the group as a whole. "Everybody set? Eddie and I will do the arraignment tomorrow, and then we get moving."

decide to spend the evening at Charlie's Sports Bar.

It may be the last chance I'll have before the intense case-preparation phase kicks in, so I might as well eat burgers, drink beer, and watch the Giants lose on *Monday Night Football*.

Vince Sanders, the editor of the local newspaper, and Pete Stanton are at our regular table when I arrive. It would take an asteroid strike to prevent their showing up, and that is only if the space rock landed directly on Charlie's.

Everything they order goes on my tab, which has been growing each week. I think they have progressed to ordering takeout for breakfast and lunch; there's no way they could be spending that much on beer and burgers only in the evenings.

Pete and I often have something of a conflict of interest. He arrests people, and I defend them. But it hasn't hurt our relationship; we are usually too busy insulting each other to focus on our respective career differences.

We don't have much time to talk before the Giants game starts, since I arrive just before kickoff. Once the game starts, we just yell at the twenty-five televisions sprinkled throughout Charlie's. Vince seems to yell at every one of the screens, as if each one bears its own responsibility for a ref's bad calls, or a Giants fumble.

At the half, the Giants are down 17–14 to the Packers, which is more competitive than I expected. Vince now has fifteen minutes not to yell at the televisions. He knows and likes Chris, so he asks me how he is doing.

"He's hanging in there. I saw him this morning."

"You're representing him?" Pete asks.

"Yes."

"I thought you were retired."

"If you would stop arresting innocent people, I would be."

"Dream on, buddy boy. This one is a stone-cold loser."

"Can I quote you on that?" Vince asks.

Pete gives Vince a menacing glare. "If you ever quote me on anything I say here, your paper will be publishing your obituary the next morning."

"Did you find a murder weapon?" I ask. Sometimes I can actually get some information from Pete between insults.

"You're confusing me with a source of defense information."

"Telling me if you have a murder weapon will help the defense? You think I won't find that out in discovery?"

Pete shrugs. "No weapon. Your boy took it with him and ditched it."

"But you couldn't find it? How inconvenient for you. Of course, the only way you can find a murder weapon is if somebody mails it to you with a note saying, 'This is the murder weapon.' And then you'd probably lose it."

"Can I quote you on that?" Vince asks me.

I try to give him the same stare that Pete did, but I

doubt mine is as menacing. "If you want to pay for your own food and beer."

Vince nods. "This conversation is completely off-the-record. They couldn't torture it out of me."

"You're a model of journalistic ethics." Then I turn to Pete. "What else can you tell me?"

"That your boy is guilty."

"The chance of you arresting an actual guilty person is too small to be measured. So what else can you tell me? I'm going to find out anyway; you're just giving me a small head start. Think of it as payment for the food and beer, or think about you two reaching for your wallets. Every. Single. Night."

"Talk to the man, Pete," Vince says, nearing panic.

"Okay. A witness heard Myers yelling at Burgess, shortly before he heard the shot. That good enough?"

I have no response to that, so I look to the TV for an escape. "Second half is starting."

take the dogs for their morning walk a little earlier than usual because I have to be in court for the arraignment.

I also want to prepare them, especially Tara, for what is to come. "I won't be around that much. You know how it is when I'm on a case."

Tara doesn't say anything, most likely because she's a dog and can't talk. But she tilts her head in that cute way she does, as if to say, *You sure you want to do this?*

Hunter doesn't seem to have a reaction; he generally lets Tara do his nontalking for him. Sebastian couldn't care less; he just wants to get home, eat, and sleep. Sebastian is living my dream, retired and loving it.

I bring them home and give them breakfast, then have my own with Laurie and Ricky. We give Ricky the great news about the spring-break trip to Disney World, and he's properly excited. He makes a face of obvious disdain when Laurie places the ear hat on his head, but fake smiles bravely.

That's my boy.

With Christmas coming up in two weeks, I'm going to have to figure out gifts to give Laurie and Ricky. The Disney trip still counts, but I need something more immediate. I have no idea what to get or where to get it . . . business as usual.

I get to court a half hour before the ten o'clock start time. The judge handling the arraignment, and probably the trial if there is one, is Susan McVay. I've never argued a case in front of her before, but she has a reputation as a no-nonsense judge. That is in direct conflict with my well-deserved reputation as a nonsense attorney.

Eddie arrives a few minutes after me, and ten minutes later the prosecution team marches in. There's only one I don't recognize, so that must be Daniel Morrow, the lead on the case. He's wearing a three-piece suit, has a new briefcase, and must have spent an hour spit shining his shoes.

He is the anti–Andy Carpenter.

He looks over and sees me, the actual Andy Carpenter, and walks over, hand extended. "Daniel Morrow."

I simultaneously shake his hand and my head. "No, Andy Carpenter."

He doesn't know what to make of that, so he just smiles. "I've heard a lot about you."

"I'm loved by pretty much all of your colleagues."

He laughs. "I must have talked to the wrong colleagues." Then, "But you and I should talk."

"Isn't that what we're doing now?"

"No, what we're doing now is exchanging insincere banter. I'm proposing we talk about something more substantive. My office this afternoon at three? Afterwards you can spend time with my colleagues who love you."

"I'll be there, but please tell them no rose petals. It's embarrassing."

Chris is brought in, and Judge McVay takes her seat at the bench moments later, putting an end to the insincere banter. The clerk announces the case; it must be jarring for Chris to hear the State of New Jersey charging him with first-degree murder, but he maintains an impassive look.

There's little to do here; we are simply setting the stage. But since I want to maintain my record of no arraignment in which I didn't lodge a complaint, I tell the judge that we are disadvantaged by not having received any discovery.

She simply turns to the prosecution table. "Mr. Morrow?"

"Your Honor, Mr. Dowd has been informed that discovery materials will start being forwarded today. I would have assumed he conveyed that news to lead counsel."

I frown. "Your Honor, simply informing us that the prosecution is not meeting their obligations does not absolve them of those obligations. It is three days and counting."

Morrow returns the frown. "Mr. Carpenter makes it sound as if three days is a long time in matters of this type."

"It only took three hours for them to rush to judgment; they must have had what they consider convincing evidence. Then we should have seen it."

"You are making the 'rush to judgment' argument already, Mr. Carpenter?" the judge asks. "There's not even a jury here."

"I'm practicing, Your Honor. But unless Mr. Morrow can say with certainty that the police have not spent the last three days looking for more evidence against Mr. Myers, then we have been seriously disadvantaged by the delay, and it is ongoing. There are four attorneys at that table; I would have to assume the xeroxing department is similarly well staffed."

Judge McVay turns to Morrow and tells him to speed up the process and report to her if there are any more delays. Morrow looks annoyed; that will teach him to call my banter insincere.

J ust curious, and you obviously don't have to tell me, but why did you complain to the judge about the discovery this morning?" I'm in Daniel Morrow's office, and he's just asked me a pretty interesting question. "I mean, you knew you were getting the discovery today, so it didn't speed things up."

The truth is I'm not sure why I raised the issue. It might have been to let everyone know we would not be pushed around. Or it might have been to get under Morrow's skin and goad him into a later mistake. Or it might be that I just like being annoying. It's probably all of the above.

"I'm a charming enigma."

"If you say so. Now, since you clearly have not had a chance to view the evidence, I don't expect you to respond, but we should talk about whether we are taking this to trial."

"Aren't trials the way we figure out winners and losers?"

"Yes, but plea bargains are another way to do it."

"What did you have in mind?"

"Well, you know how this works around here probably better than I do, so you know I am not calling the shots. I think I can get forty years, with possible parole after thirty."

"Forty years? The Giants might win another Super Bowl before then."

"They have televisions inside the prison," Morrow says. "He won't miss a thing."

"What about the eight-hour pregame show? Would they let him watch that? That's when they run some of the best commercials."

"So you're not interested?" Just like earlier today, Morrow does not seem all that impressed by my enigmatic charm.

"Wouldn't matter either way; it's up to my client to be interested or not. He's the one who'd be listening to Tony Romo behind bars, not me. It's my job to give him my opinion and let him decide."

"You want to share your opinion?"

"I thought you'd never ask. Chris Myers is innocent of this crime. I haven't seen the evidence, but it doesn't matter what it shows, because it's horseshit. If I were in his position, I would think that there could be reasons to throw my life away, but horseshit evidence isn't one of them."

"I've never tried a case against an enigma before; should be interesting."

"I can promise that."

I leave Morrow's office and head down to the jail. Even though he said he needed final permission to make the offer he described, I'm going to treat it as a definite offer. He wouldn't have mentioned it if he couldn't deliver it. In any event, based on the seriousness of the crime and Chris's previous record, the final offer is definitely not going to be much better, and it could be worse.

I only have to wait ten minutes before Chris is brought into the interview room. "You bring any good news?" he asks without preamble.

"Afraid not. You'll know when and if I have any; I'll be wearing what Laurie calls my shit-eating grin."

"I'll look forward to it."

"The prosecution made a tentative plea offer, though we can treat it as definite. Forty years, possible parole in thirty."

He sits back in the chair, clearly stunned. "I can't do that." Then, "Actually, there's no offer they could make that I would take. I've gone to prison once for a crime I didn't commit. . . . Been there, done that."

"Okay."

"What are our chances?"

"I have no idea; I won't get to see any of the evidence until tonight." Then, "Do you own a gun?"

He shakes his head. "No. I never have and couldn't now if I wanted to. I'm a convicted felon."

"When you left Burgess's house, did you see anyone?"

"I'm not sure. I don't recall anyone, but there could have been someone there and I might not have noticed. I wasn't thinking too clearly, and I was scared on two levels. One that I might get shot, and two that I might get blamed. At this point I think I might have been better off getting shot."

"How much do you know about Burgess?"

"Not much. Just that he was a lying piece of garbage."

"How long have you been sober, Chris?"

"Since I went to prison the first time; haven't had a drink since."

"So no alcohol in your system the night Burgess died? That's for sure?"

Chris nods vehemently . . . the very question seems to aggravate him. "That is one hundred percent for sure."

I leave Chris and see a text on my cell from Eddie Dowd, telling me the discovery has been delivered to my house. I'll be reading it tonight, which means that listening to that insufferable Christmas music will be the high point of the evening.

The discovery is as bad as anticipated, and in one way excruciatingly worse.

In the prosecution version of it, they know forensically that Chris was in the house; they have his fingerprints to prove it.

They have a witness who saw him leave the house in a hurry. That person will also testify to having heard an argument between the two men, and then a gunshot, both just before Chris left.

They also have a copy of the brief we filed and withdrew, referring to Burgess's upcoming recanting of his earlier testimony. Devastatingly, there is an interview with Richard Wallace, recounting that I told him Burgess had changed his mind and Chris was upset about it and going to talk with him.

The bottom line is that I provided the prosecution with incontrovertible motive evidence, both with the brief and my conversation with Richard. There was nothing confidential about that conversation; Richard was perfectly correct to reveal it.

But there is no doubt about it; my actions inadvertently contributed to a probable disaster for my client.

They would have focused on the motive anyway, but I gave them a road map.

"You know you did the right thing," Laurie says.

"Actually, I don't. I rushed it because Chris was anxious to get it done. I should have confirmed for myself that Burgess was set."

"He set the terms. He said he wouldn't deal with anyone but Chris and would only tell his story once. He even bailed out without you intervening."

"You're trying to make me feel better."

She nods. "Guilty as charged. But this time I'm also right. Now let's talk about the case."

"That will make me even more depressed."

"Burgess is our first key. If Burgess lied the first time, we have to assume he was put up to it. He told Chris that he was paid, and Chris said he seemed afraid of the people who paid him. So we need to find out who they are, and why they did what they did."

I nod. "And it would fit into that theory that the same person or persons killed him. Maybe they didn't know he had ultimately decided not to recant, or maybe they just viewed him as a dangerous loose end."

"Right. And the other key is why they did this to Chris. Why did they want him out of the way and in jail?"

"But basically we're talking about the first time; that's when they wanted him gone. That may be true this time as well, but more likely not."

"Why do you say that?" she asks.

"I've got a feeling this was more about killing Burgess than framing Chris. The killer wouldn't even have known that Chris was going to Burgess's house. I think Chris was somehow dangerous to them back then, but probably not now."

"So we have our two-pronged approach."

"Yes," I say. "Unless the truth is that Chris went to Burgess's house, got pissed off that he wasn't going to testify, and shot him."

"You think that's possible?"

"I told Morrow it isn't, that Chris is definitely innocent. But do I know that for a fact? No."

"Innocent or guilty, he's entitled to the same defense," she says.

"I had a law professor who used to say that all the time; I hated that guy."

"But it's true."

"In theory, yes. But he won't be able to benefit from that defense if he's guilty. Because the things we just said are the keys to this, the questions we have to answer . . . none of that will wind up in our favor. We won't find the guy who paid Burgess off if Burgess wasn't paid off."

"Did your law professor say that also?"

"He may have mentioned it on one of the days I cut class."

"Doesn't matter," she says. "Because I don't think Chris did it, and down deep in that gut you actually trust, you don't either."

"Why don't you think so?"

"Because I know him, and I do not see him shooting an unarmed man at point-blank range. I don't think he has it in him."

"The prosecution position will be that he has an uncontrollable temper, that he just snaps. They'll say it happened twice, and two people are dead because of it."

Laurie shakes her head in disagreement. "It doesn't compute. I don't believe he owned a gun; as a convicted felon that in itself would be a crime. Why would he have one and risk going back to prison? To go duck hunting? But more importantly, he wouldn't have brought a gun to Burgess's house unless he at least entertained the prospect of using it."

"True."

"Which argues against uncontrollable rage; it would have been premeditated, or at least contemplated. But the other point is that shooting Burgess would have been entirely counterproductive. He was the only one who could clear Chris. Why kill him? Even if he refused to testify, there was always the possibility he could change his mind. He certainly showed a tendency for that. Once he was dead, so was Chris's chance to be exonerated."

Laurie is right . . . she has pointed out the errors in my thinking.

I hate that.

Keith Richter recognized exactly how well things were going for him, and he took none of it for granted.

At thirty-one he was already an associate professor in nuclear physics at MIT and was a protégé of the man who resided near the top of the field. Richter was making excellent money for a man his age, but nowhere near what he was about to make.

Richter was a near genius in his field, but not an actual genius. He knew that because he had a true genius to compare himself to, and that was his boss, Professor Clifford Heyer. But that was okay, Richter was comfortable and enjoying life, both in academia and outside it.

Thirty-one was the perfect age socially for Richter. He wasn't too old for the female graduate students at MIT, or even some of the older undergrads. They even respected his position; he was doing better with women than he ever had before, though Keith would have been the first to admit that it was not a high bar to scale.

He knew that once he was wealthy, he would have to discipline himself to continue to climb the academic ladder. He had always been good about that, and he felt he'd continue on that path. He enjoyed the work, and financial security would not change that.

So the pressure was off socially, and soon to be off financially. This particular night reflected that. He went out for a drink and dinner, by himself, at a popular hangout off campus. He had an early meeting the next morning and wanted to make it an early night.

So he was friendly to everyone there, but didn't have much interest in joining a group, or hooking up with anyone for the night. That by itself was a good feeling.

Keith headed home at a little after nine. He'd watch the Celtic game in bed and probably watch the first half of the Laker game after that. That would still allow him a good night's sleep, so that he could be fresh in the morning.

Keith's apartment was six blocks away, an easy walk. But that night the walk was not quite so easy. Halfway home, three men appeared out of the shadows and grabbed him. One put his hand over Keith's mouth to prevent him from yelling out.

Almost instantly a car pulled up, and Keith was shoved into the back seat, bookended by two of the men. The car drove off with Keith and his four assailants.

"What's going on?" Keith was petrified at what had just happened. "You must have me confused with someone else." Down deep, though, he knew that wasn't true.

The man in the passenger seat turned around. "You thought you could force your way in? You thought you could be a part of this?"

Keith instantly knew what the man was talking about and switched into escape mode. "I don't have to be; I just took a shot. If it's a problem, I'll back off. I just thought I could help."

"We don't need your help."

"Okay, I understand now. Let me out and I won't cause any problems, I promise. You'll never hear another word from me."

The man smiled. "You got that right."

Two days later, Keith Richter, his lifeless body broken at the neck, was found in the Charles River.

've called a meeting for later this morning so the team can update me on anything we have learned about Charlie Burgess.

First I'm heading down to the Tara Foundation. If puppies can't get me out of my funk, nothing can. I bring Tara with me; she seems mesmerized by them, as if she can't believe they can be that small.

"They're doing great," says Sondra. "And they're so cute we could have placed them ten times over if we wanted to. One guy was in here and saw them; he wanted to take two for his girlfriend, to surprise her."

"Uh-oh. Was Willie here when he said it?"

She laughs. "He was. I was afraid he was going to get into it with the guy, but I calmed him down. It could have gotten ugly."

"Nice going. I don't need another client." Willie can be aggressively protective of the dogs in our care, and he's not about to watch them be reduced to a Christmas present.

After about twenty minutes, Tara seems to have had enough of the puppies crawling all over her. Killian, their mother, seems grateful for the respite, but Tara is like a grandmother who gets to enjoy the kids and then go home.

Of course, Tara is getting to go home to take a nap on

the couch. I've got to stay awake and hear about Charlie Burgess.

Corey and Sam are over to brief Laurie and me on what they've come up with. Marcus has done a lot of the legwork, but he's updated Corey on it for this meeting. Marcus is not real big on meetings.

Sam starts it off. "Burgess was convicted twice of passing bad checks. He had a third arrest for running numbers, but it was dropped. Not sure why.

"The guy had a somewhat checkered history with money; he certainly couldn't hang on to any. Six years ago he actually won thirty-five grand on one of those scratch-off lotteries, but it didn't last. Then about two and a half years ago he made three cash deposits in his account of nine grand each. That also didn't last.

"He was never married, no family that I can find except some cousins in Massachusetts who he didn't seem to have any contact with, at least not by telephone. He lived in the same house for fifteen years." Sam shrugs. "That's about it."

"Any way of finding out where he got the cash?" I know what Sam is going to say, but I am asking the question just in case.

"Not from the banking records."

"The timing works for a payoff for testifying against Chris," Laurie says.

I nod. "Right."

Corey goes next. "Maybe he had a rare lucky streak. According to Marcus, he was a degenerate gambler, and not a good one. He was always scrounging for money."

"Who was his bookmaker?"

"Jimmy Dinardo."

"Ah, Jimmy," I say. "We've chatted with him a few times. Maybe we will again."

"Whatever was going on, Burgess was not a key player," Corey says. "He was small-time all the way."

"Did he have a job?"

"Officially? He worked for the post office for a while, then did some construction work. Unofficially, he probably did whatever was needed. But nothing big. He would have been a perfect guy to recruit to lie about the death."

"Any close friends we can talk to?"

"Not that Marcus knows of yet. He did say that Burgess used to go every night to the bar where the death took place."

"That continued on until recently?" Laurie asks.

Corey nods. "Apparently. Marcus also found out who the bartender was that night back then, and he's still there. Works every weeknight; his name is Ray Kendall."

"He testified at the trial." I turn to Laurie. "How'd you like a night out on the town? You can dress fancy and drink as much beer as you like."

She smiles. "You really know how to turn a girl's head."

Corey turns to Laurie. "You want me to come along?"

"No need," I say. "I can protect her if anything goes down. If I have to protect you as well, I might be stretched too thin."

Corey nods. "You've been stretched too thin for a while."

Laurie says, "If I get scared, I'll just hide behind Andy."

The Basement Bar is in downtown Paterson, off Market Street.

Its name is half-accurate, in that it actually is a bar. But it's not in the basement; maybe the person that named it spent too much time in the bar and wasn't thinking clearly.

It's not quite street level either; you go down two steps to get to the door. Once Laurie and I enter, it becomes apparent that the altitude doesn't matter; it's like every crummy bar you've ever been in. Even crummier.

Maybe a dozen people are here, most of whom look like they have been in place for a while and don't have immediate plans to leave. These people are not having a drink before leaving for an Adele concert, and no business deals are being discussed. This is a destination bar; no one is on the way back from somewhere or heading to somewhere.

Near the back are two bumper-pool tables, which elevates the place in my eyes. Back in the day I was the self-proclaimed NYU bumper-pool champion, and seeing the tables makes me want to throw down the gauntlet and challenge all comers. I don't, because these people don't seem the type to be intimidated by gauntlet throwing; they might even have concealed-gauntlet permits.

Laurie takes one look around and says, "This is the place Chris came to drink?"

I just shrug; I don't understand it and make plans to ask him. There is no doubt that when Chris went to prison, the Basement Bar immediately lost 100 percent of their New York law firm crowd.

We walk over to the bar. The one bartender, who I hope is Ray Kendall, is serving a beer to a guy at the other end. He finishes and sees us, but washes some glasses instead. I'm not sure why he is ignoring us, but he has succeeded in getting on my nerves without saying a word.

"Hey," I say, a clever conversation starter. It doesn't work, so I say it again.

He finally frowns and comes over to us. "Yeah? What are you drinking?"

"I'll have a sarsaparilla, straight up," I say. "And one for my friend here."

"What the hell are you talking about?"

Laurie talks to Kendall while rolling her eyes at me. She's a multitasker. "Are you Ray Kendall?"

"Yeah. What are you drinking?"

"We're not. We're interested in Charlie Burgess."

"Too late. He's dead."

"He used to come in here all the time?"

"Yeah. And now he don't."

"*Doesn't,*" I say. "And now he *doesn't.* That's because *he* is singular."

"You're getting on my nerves," Kendall says.

"You just cost yourself a big tip. You were here the night Joey Bonaventura was killed."

"Yeah. Who are you two?"

"We're private investigators," Laurie says. "Why did you say that Chris Myers and Bonaventura were arguing?"

"Because they were."

"What about?"

"Who cares? They were drunk."

"Why would Burgess lie about what he saw?" I ask.

"He wouldn't."

"He had gambling debts," I say.

"So?"

"So who paid him to lie so the debts would go away? Maybe the same person who paid you to say they argued?"

This obviously annoys him. "I got nothing to say to you."

Two guys at the end of the bar, both in their thirties, seem to be taking an interest in our conversation. I'm not sure if Laurie has noticed them, but if I have, it's likely that she has as well.

"Burgess have any friends we could talk to?" I ask. "Like anyone that might be here at the moment?"

"No one's going to talk to you," Kendall says. "Including me, starting now. So beat it; I'm busy."

"Let's go." Laurie turns and walks slowly toward the door. I see the two guys get up as well; again, I'm not positive Laurie does.

Before I follow her, I say to Kendall, "Don't try and charge us for the sarsaparillas."

When we get outside, she says, "This way," and starts walking to the right. That seems a bit strange, because the car is to the left.

"Where are we going?"

My question apparently isn't worthy of a response.

We turn at the end of the street, then turn again into the back alley. Laurie puts her fingers to her mouth in a gesture for me to be quiet, and she tucks us into an area behind a column sticking out from one of the buildings. It's fairly dark back here; the only light is coming from lights inside the buildings, with little moonlight.

I hear footsteps; it doesn't take a top-notch detective to know that it is the two guys from the bar. They can't see us, and for the moment we can't see them. A few seconds later, they walk past us, and I hear one of them say, "Where the hell did they go?"

"You looking for us?" Laurie asks.

They turn and see the gun in her hand at the same time I do.

One of them is considerably bigger than the other, but neither is particularly petite. The smaller guy says, "Hey." I don't think it has any particular meaning; he probably just couldn't think of anything else to say.

"Why were you following us?" Laurie asks.

"That's bullshit. We were just walking."

"If I hear one more word that I don't like out of your mouth, I am going to shoot you in both kneecaps, and you'll be using a walker for the rest of your pathetic life."

I have a feeling I did not marry a delicate flower.

"Okay," bigger guy says. "Everybody's cool here."

"So I'll ask the question one more time. Why were you following us?"

"Because you were asking questions about Charlie Burgess. Charlie was a friend of ours."

I realize that I have not said a word since we left the bar;

it's time to rectify that. "And now we're going to ask some more questions. Who killed him?"

"Don't know."

"Not a good answer," I say. "I don't think you realize how much danger you're in here."

"Charlie knew some bad people. We don't know who they are, but he was afraid of them."

"Why?"

"Because they kill people. He was leaving town."

"Why did he lie about the killing behind the bar?" As I'm saying it, I realize that we are standing almost exactly where it took place.

"Money. Charlie owed a lot of money. They gave him all he needed, and everything was cool. But he must have pissed them off."

"What can you tell us about them?"

"Nothing, I swear," bigger guy says. "Charlie thought he was through with them. But then something happened to bring them back. That's why he was leaving."

"You ever see them?"

"No," bigger guy says, and smaller guy chimes in with "Me neither."

I'm running out of stuff to ask them, and not terribly hopeful of getting any more information anyway. "You said Charlie owed money from gambling?"

Smaller guy nods. "Yeah, always. If Charlie bet the sun was going to come up tomorrow, it would be dark all day."

"Did a lot of people know about that?"

"Yeah. Charlie talked about it all the time. You couldn't be around him without hearing about it. He always got robbed on every bet; he thought the refs were out to get him personally."

"Okay. Start walking down the alley that way," Laurie says. "If you turn around, even once, it will be the worst mistake you ever made."

They do exactly as they are told, and we walk the other way. Laurie walks backward, so she can keep an eye on them.

Within a couple of minutes, we're in the car and driving away.

"We showed them," I say.

What the hell were you doing in that bar in the first place?" I ask, moments after Chris is brought into the meeting room. "It's a complete dump."

"You went down there?"

"I did. Laurie and I made quite an impression. It's not a place I would picture you hanging out."

"No, but it's a place where I could be anonymous, where I wouldn't be seen by anyone I worked with. I could drink without worrying about running into anybody from that part of my world. And believe me, the alcohol tastes the same as it does at the Carlyle. Maybe watered down a bit, but if you drink enough, you can compensate for that."

"Did you know Charlie Burgess before that night?"

"Depends what you mean by *know*. He was there all the time, but we weren't friends. He talked a lot, and before I had enough drinks in me to shut out the noise, I listened. It was hard not to."

"Did he talk about his gambling losses?"

"All the time."

"What about Joey Bonaventura, the guy who died? Did you know him before that night?"

"No. I literally never saw him, including that night.

I was there, went home, and the police came and arrested me."

"The bartender said you were arguing with Bonaventura before you went outside."

"He's either mistaken or lying. I'd bet on lying."

"So it's not possible?"

"Andy, I was drunk. Could I have argued with someone and not remembered? I guess it's possible. Could I have gotten in a fight, killed a guy, and forgotten about it? That is not possible."

"How did you get home?"

"Must have been a taxi. They always called me one . . . even I wasn't dumb enough to drive."

"Who would have called it?"

"The bartender."

It's surprising to me that neither the prosecution nor defense followed up on this in the first trial. Chris could have said something either incriminating or exculpatory to the cabbie, but no one made any attempt to track it down.

"Okay," I say. "Now this is important. If these people are lying, and were paid to do so, then someone very badly wanted you out of the way. We need to figure out the who and why."

"I can't imagine. I didn't think I had any enemies that could come anywhere near doing something like this."

"Maybe they weren't enemies."

"What do you mean?"

"Maybe just your being out of the picture helped them somehow. Could it have had to do with your work?"

"I don't know how."

"Think about it. Try and remember all the things you were involved in; write down everything that comes to mind."

"Okay."

"And who at your firm should I talk to?"

"About what I was working on?"

"Yes."

He thinks for a few moments. "It would have to be Vic Everson . . . Victor Everson . . . he is the managing partner."

"Were you and he on good terms?"

"Well, he fired me, so there is that, but believe me, after my arrest, he had no choice. Alcoholic felons are really not highly sought after by law firms. But he always tried to be supportive; he was sort of a mentor to me. I think he'd be at least somewhat sympathetic and helpful. He's a good guy."

"Okay, I'll start with him."

"I wasn't working on the kind of stuff that could lead to something like this."

"You're probably right, but we have to check all the boxes."

Chris nods. "I'll start working on it, but it's a long time ago. I haven't thought about that stuff for a very long time."

"It's important."

"I understand. How are the puppies doing?"

"They set new adorableness records every day."

"Maybe you can save one for me if we win?"

"I can do that."

"Are we going to win?" His expression is hopeful, but

he's cringing at the same time. It's a look that every client I've ever had adopts at one time or another.

I never lie to my clients when they ask this question, and they almost always ask this question. "At this point I don't have the slightest idea."

"When do you usually know?"

"When the clerk reads the verdict."

t's not a stretch to believe that the bartender would lie," Laurie says. "He did not strike me as a model of morality."

"No question. But he would only lie for one of two reasons; either A, he was getting paid to do it, or B, he was afraid not to."

"Or he just found you annoying."

"Come on, be serious. I was thoroughly charming. You were there; I even trotted out my impish smile."

"Well, in this case, if I was voting for the most likely reason he lied, I would say C, all of the above."

"Why?"

"Because at the time, he was supporting Burgess's lie, and Burgess was getting paid. There's no reason to think that whoever was paying Burgess wouldn't pay the bartender also."

"You said C, all of the above," I point out.

"Right, because in telling us that he doesn't know anything, he's lying now. And he has good reason for fear to be a motivation; he's seen what happened to Burgess."

I nod. "Right. And those guys in the alley were sure of one thing: that the people we are dealing with are dangerous and scary."

"So they're using all that money and all that scariness to put Chris Myers in jail? Is that our theory?"

"Not quite. I think that's what they did the first time; I'm not so sure about this time. I still think that Chris being present when they killed Burgess may have been just a convenient coincidence for them. They would have had no way of knowing he was going to be there."

"So they wanted him out of the way then, but not now?"

"That's very possible. Which means he was a threat then, but isn't anymore."

"What's the difference between him now and then?"

"The only thing I can think of is his job," I say. "I have a meeting with his boss in the morning; maybe I'll learn more then."

"I hope so." Then, "You'd better hurry up and get dressed."

"For what?"

"The holiday party at Ricky's school. I did tell you about it, Andy."

"Oh, no . . . you told me about it weeks ago; I never thought it would actually get here."

"You were hoping the holidays would get called off in the meantime?"

"That was just one of the possibilities I was rooting for, and it was way down on the list."

"Well, none of them came to pass. And act happy; Ricky is really looking forward to it."

"Any chance I can use work as an excuse?"

"Zero."

So, wimp that I am, I change out of my jeans and sweatshirt and put on clothes more appropriate for the party.

Ricky does seem anxious to go; it's hard to believe I had a hand in raising this child.

The party is in the school gym. There's tinsel everywhere, hanging from the ceiling and the backboard and rims on the court. The food is spread out on one table; it consists of pieces of what is either cheese or Formica, along with carrots and celery. The liquid in the punch bowl is interesting; it's as if they couldn't decide whether to have eggnog or fruit punch, so they split the difference. Think grape juice that oozes, rather than pours.

At least fifty people wish me a merry Christmas; I have no idea who forty-eight of them are and am only guessing at the other two. After about an hour, the school principal gets up and gives a warm holiday speech, followed by the real reason we're stuck here: they want to raise funds for school field trips.

I write the check and we're out of here.

The Everson, Manning & Winkler law firm is about as far as you can get from the Basement Bar and still be on the same planet.

The offices, which are on Central Park South between Sixth and Seventh Avenues, were designed by someone who must have been operating under a clear directive: make the place look classy and expensive, and don't worry about how many mahoganies you kill in the process.

I'm here to see Victor Everson, who Chris described as something of a mentor, at least until Everson fired him. Everson had taken my call immediately, and while he didn't see how he could help, he was willing to give me some of his time.

The elevator takes me to the thirty-eighth floor, which makes sense, since I had pressed 38. It's high-speed, which is a trait I admire in elevators, and I'm up there so fast I am surprised to see the number 38 when the door opens.

A big, fully decorated Christmas tree is in the reception area. I'm willing to bet that neither Everson, Manning, nor Winkler put on the ornaments and strung the lights; I'm sure they hired someone. I would suggest that to Laurie for our own tree next year, but she might string me up if I did.

One of the three receptionists checks her list to confirm

that I do have an appointment to see Mr. Everson. I must be on that list because she makes a call and a young woman comes out to lead me back to Everson's office.

Victor Everson is sitting behind his desk when I arrive. His back is to a glass wall, through which there is an amazing view of Central Park. The huge rectangle of green is cut out of a larger rectangle of cement and high-rise buildings.

He gets up and comes around his desk to greet me, and we shake hands, but I cannot take my eyes off that view. "That would be enough to get me to come to work every day. Or at least most days."

He turns around and looks at it as well. "It is definitely a perk of the job. But there are actually some people who are afraid of heights and get nervous being up here."

"Not me. I'm afraid of lows."

We sit down and I decline his offer of something to drink. "So, you wanted to talk about Chris." He shakes his head in apparent sadness. "The biggest disappointment of my professional life."

"Have you had many?"

"Of course. You're a lawyer; you know that occasional defeats are part of the job."

"One of the reasons to leave the job. What kind of law does your firm practice?"

"Might be easier to list what we don't practice. We don't do criminal, for one, or family, for another. We do litigation of all types; Chris was an excellent litigator, until he wasn't."

"I'm interested in knowing what he was working on at the time he was terminated."

"Why don't you ask him?"

"I have. But his recall may not be one hundred percent."

"I can imagine. Chris was having a difficult time in those days. I'm sure you must know that."

"He was drinking heavily."

"Yes. I tried to get him to deal with it, as did several of his colleagues. Chris was well-liked here, especially by me. And he was extremely talented. He would no doubt have made partner by now, if . . ."

Everson doesn't finish the thought; he doesn't have to. Instead, he asks, "So what can I do?"

"The business he was working on . . ."

"I'm afraid I can't help you much there. For one thing, I don't know; I would have to research it. But more significantly, and I know you understand this, I can't discuss our clients' business with anyone outside the firm."

"I'm not asking for confidential information."

"That would open a door that might be difficult to close. Let me put it this way; if Chris tells you about something he was working on, you can ask me a specific question about it. If it is something I'm comfortable answering, I will."

I'm not happy about this; seems to me like Everson is willing to do whatever he can to help Chris, except for actually helping Chris.

"Who took on Chris's clients when he left?"

Everson shrugs. "Sorry, can't go there."

"Let me see if I understand this, because maybe I cut class in law school the day this came up. I'm representing Chris Myers as his attorney. If you speak to me, you are speaking to him. Are you saying that telling Chris what he was working on violates some rule of confidentiality?"

"I don't see it the way you do."

"Clearly."

"Is there anything else I can do for you?"

"No, I wouldn't want to spoil your record."

"I have a responsibility to my clients."

I nod. "Don't we all."

Laurie and I always visit murder scenes together; it's one of those cute little romantic quirks, the kind that all couples share.

Sometimes I wonder that if there were no more murders, what would we do for entertainment? Laurie doesn't care much for sports, and you'd have to strap me down to watch ballet or opera, or to listen to classical music.

Murder scenes are the one thing we can do together; my eyes fill with tears as I think about it.

In this case two criminal deaths are relevant to our case. One, obviously, is the Charlie Burgess killing, which Chris stands accused of. The other is the Joey Bonaventura manslaughter case, which Chris was convicted of, and which caused him to serve time.

We have already visited the Bonaventura scene, which took place behind the Basement Bar. That's where we confronted the two friends of Burgess's who followed us back there.

We didn't study the area; Laurie was too busy dealing with those guys, and I was way too busy watching her. But since it's been almost three years since the event, there was little to learn anyway. All the diagrams and descriptions of the place that we could want are in the trial transcript.

The Burgess scene is something else. For one thing, it's fresher . . . not that we're going to find trace evidence left behind. But the scene has not been analyzed to death, at least not by someone who isn't intent on putting Chris away for the rest of his life.

Burgess lived in a modest house in Totowa, a small borough adjacent to Paterson. It's just about four square miles in size and has about ten thousand people. Charlie Burgess was not one of the more prominent citizens of Totowa.

My only connection to Totowa actually isn't one at all. As a kid I played baseball at a field called Totowa Oval, which is in Paterson and not Totowa. I thought that was strange, until the New York Giants and the New York Jets started playing their games in East Rutherford, New Jersey.

Burgess's house is at the end of a dead-end street, which means that there is only a neighbor on the left side, as you face the house. I'm assuming that Chris entered through a window on the right side, since his prints were found there at an open window.

Chris had readily admitted to me that he entered through a bedroom window when Burgess didn't answer repeated pounding on the door. According to the discovery, the back door was slightly ajar as well, which could work in our favor.

We don't have to enter through a window, which is just as well, since it would take a crane to get me up to it. There is still a police presence on the scene, and they have been notified to let us in. The cop at the front door does so, but forgets to smile.

Once inside, we take our time looking around. Chris said he ran out through the front door, which makes perfect sense. He was afraid that the killer was still in the house with him, so he had no time or inclination to climb back out through the window, especially since the killer might have entered the same way.

The downside to this, which he could not have known, was that a neighbor saw him leave in a hurry, soon after hearing the gunshot.

Burgess was shot in the den. The way the house is laid out, it's the first room that Chris would have entered after coming through the bedroom window.

The dreaded chalk marks on the floor, as well as the remaining bloodstains, leave no doubt as to where Burgess was when he was shot.

"I know we believe this already, but Chris is not the killer," Laurie says, obviously seeing and understanding something that I have not picked up on.

"Why do you say that?"

"Because if he came through the window and entered this room, Burgess would have looked at him. Both Chris and the witness said they argued. You look at someone when you're arguing, especially someone who just broke into your house.

"Yet according to the discovery, the bullet entered the side of his head. Burgess would not have looked away, especially if Chris was holding or grabbing a gun."

"The prosecution would say that Chris surprised him and shot him before Burgess even knew he was there."

Laurie shakes her head. "No, they won't, because of the witness describing the argument. But we know it couldn't have happened that way. Chris was not there to kill him; he was there to convince him to testify. The one sure way to prevent that testimony would be to sneak up on him and shoot him in the head."

"This is why I bring you to murder scenes. When I used to bring other dates to these things, they'd go, 'Oooh, blood . . . how icky.'"

"You dated women who said 'icky'?"

"Almost exclusively." Then, "So if he was shot in the left side of the head and the body was here, the shot had to come from over there."

I walk to the place where the killer must have stood, then turn and walk down the hall. "The killer could easily have come in the back door, walked down here, shot Burgess, and then gone out the same way. And if he was in the doorway, Chris probably wouldn't have seen him."

Laurie nods. "Absolutely makes sense."

"Makes sense to us, but wouldn't to a jury. The reason we buy it is that we go into it believing Chris is innocent. The jury would think he snuck up on Burgess and shot him from the side when he turned his head. Coming through a window is consistent with that; that's not how people usually enter a house."

We walk to the back and see residue of the material they use to detect fingerprints. Chris's were not found there, which does nothing to negatively impact the prosecution's case, since they were found on the window. Since he only entered the house once, they don't need two entry points, and the window entry is much more incriminating.

We go through the back door to the yard. Another set of houses is beyond that, which are on the next street over.

"The killer could have parked there, come in through the back door, and then gone out the same way, through the yard to his car," she says.

"And it also could have been done without his even knowing Chris was there."

She shakes her head. "I doubt that. He must have known someone was there because Burgess and Chris argued loudly, and the killer would have heard it."

"Let's say he discovered Chris was there when he got inside. He didn't shoot Chris, obviously, but there could have been two reasons for that. One is so he could blame him for the shooting, but I doubt that was it. The other, more likely one, is that he didn't care about Chris one way or the other. He may not even have known who Chris was. His goal was to kill Burgess and get out; Chris wouldn't have been important to him. It all fits."

"The jury will wonder why the killer would have left Chris alive, since Chris could conceivably identify him. I know I would wonder that myself."

"Why do you have to say stuff like that and ruin things?" I ask. "We were having so much fun."

Jimmy Dinardo is an independent contractor, although that depends on your definition of *independent*.

There are two kinds of bookmakers in North Jersey: the ones who work for the family of Joseph Russo Jr. and the ones who don't. But even the ones who don't must still pay tribute, a portion of their profits, to Joe Jr.

In return, they get three things. One, they are allowed to operate. Two, they are allowed to continue living. And three, if they get so much action on one side of a game that it makes them uncomfortable, they can lay some off with Russo's people.

That probably requires some explanation. Bookmakers aren't gamblers; their goal is to have an equal amount of money bet on both sides, so their profit is the percentage they take off the top, called vig. If too much money is coming in on one side, they adjust the betting line to encourage more betting on the other side.

If that doesn't work, and the betting is still heavily weighted to one side or the other, then people like Dinardo can call Russo's people and lay some of it off, thereby spreading the risk. For Dinardo and those like him, it is a way to avert a potential disaster.

Based on what Marcus has learned, Dinardo was pretty

much the most important person in Charlie Burgess's life. Burgess by any definition was a degenerate gambler, so Dinardo was the drug that satisfied Burgess's addiction.

I've had some experience with Dinardo on a previous case. Marcus and I went to see him, and he gave us some information that we needed. People tend to give Marcus whatever he wants, whenever he wants it.

We badly need to learn whatever we can about Burgess, and since he doesn't have a Wikipedia page, we're reduced to talking to people like Dinardo. Of course, people like Dinardo don't like to talk to people like me, so once again I am bringing along the aforementioned Marcus.

Generally, when I am going to be in any kind of potentially dangerous situation, Laurie insists on coming along, and often Corey does as well. They don't think I can handle myself if violence breaks out, and I have in the past given them ample reason to feel that way. But they don't have that same concern when I am going to be with Marcus.

We know from past experience that Dinardo works out of a small office off Bergen Street in Paterson, in what amounts to little more than an alley. While I doubt he's a military tactician, in this setup his bodyguards can see and intercept anyone coming. Since Dinardo often has a lot of cash on him, and since he's not under Russo Jr.'s protection, there could be an attempt to rip him off.

Marcus has reconfirmed the location, so we're going to see Dinardo tonight. Whenever I am in situations like this, I get nervous, but having Marcus calms me. Of course, if I didn't have Marcus, I'd be even calmer, because I wouldn't be going in the first place.

Marcus picks me up, as planned, at 10:00 P.M. For many years I thought that Marcus only spoke in unintelligible grunts, and very little of that. I have since learned otherwise; he speaks absolutely normally when he wants to. But he rarely wants to, and he says almost nothing the entire way to Dinardo's.

For all of Marcus's incredible prowess in violent encounters, he is careful. He plans things to minimize risk and maximize the chance of success, then deals with whatever comes along.

In this case, while the alley to the door of Dinardo's office is fairly long, the office is not in the middle. It is much closer to one end. Marcus parks on the street at the farther end, so that the car is less likely to be heard or noticed by Dinardo's people.

Then we walk around the block and enter the alley on the shorter side, giving them less chance to react when they do see us. It's dark, and we're quiet, so we should be able to get close before we're noticed. The only danger is if they hear my heart pounding, which is a distinct possibility.

I walk a full step behind Marcus, sort of the way people treat Queen Elizabeth. I do it out of fear; in situations like this I am a follower, not a leader. I find it hard to maintain my dignity, but at least I refuse to curtsy.

When we turn the corner into the alley, Marcus picks up the pace considerably, and I keep up behind him. Before the two bodyguards outside Dinardo's office realize what's happened, we're upon them.

I recognize one of them from last time. The other, much larger, one is a newcomer, at least as far as I am concerned.

"Hey." It's the guy from last time speaking and registering his surprise.

"Good evening. Remember us?" I say.

"No, I . . . ," last-time guy starts, then looks at Marcus. "Oh, shit . . . yeah, I remember."

I'm actually surprised at his ability to recall our last meeting, since he had stupidly challenged Marcus and wound up unconscious for his trouble.

"Good," I say. "Same situation as last time. We want to talk to Jimmy."

"Nobody talks to Jimmy," the new big guy says.

"You probably should explain the situation to him," I say to last-time guy.

He nods. "Rock, these guys are okay . . . let 'em go."

"His name is Rock?" I ask. "Seriously? Rock? Like short for Rocky?"

"Nobody talks to Jimmy," Rock repeats. "Beat it." He walks toward us.

Marcus does nothing, just stands there, until Rock reaches out his arm to grab Marcus. Obviously Rock is not short for Rocky, it's short for Rocks for Brains.

I can't see Marcus move; it's dark and he's quick. But he must have moved because I hear the thud of fist hitting gut, a beautiful sound, and suddenly Rock is on the ground, moaning and gagging.

Last-time guy looks at Rock, then says to us, "Jimmy's inside."

O h, shit," Jimmy Dinardo says when he sees us enter the room.

"That is exactly what your colleague at the door said," I say. "We're not feeling the love here."

"They just let you in?"

I shrug. "There was some resistance on the part of Rock, but it was resolved quickly enough."

"He's a moron," Jimmy says.

"Blame his parents. You name your kid Rock, you're not telling him you're thinking there's a PhD in his future."

"What do you want this time?"

"Same as last time. We just want to have a little talk."

"What about?"

"Charlie Burgess."

"The son of a bitch died owing me six grand."

"Jimmy, your problem is that you are too sentimental. It won't serve you well in the long run."

"What the hell are you talking about?"

"I told you . . . Charlie Burgess. We have some questions, you no doubt have some answers, and then we're on our way."

Jimmy looks frustrated. I'm sure he's pissed off also,

but probably afraid to antagonize Marcus. "Ask the damn questions."

"You said he died owing you six grand; what's the most he ever owed you?"

"What am I, a damn accountant? Maybe twenty-five. Yeah, twenty-five."

"When was that?"

"A few years ago."

"But he paid it?"

Dinardo smiles. "Yeah, you might say that."

"That's a little cryptic for me, Jimmy."

He looks puzzled. "What does that mean?"

"Never mind. How did he get the money to pay the twenty-five grand?"

"Two guys showed up one day; I think they were connected, but I didn't ask and it didn't matter. They asked me some questions about Burgess, how much he owed, what kind of guy he was, could he be trusted, that kind of stuff.

"They gave me five grand for answering their questions, and for keeping my mouth shut about them. They also told me Charlie would be paying the twenty-five."

"But you didn't keep your mouth shut about them, you just told us."

"Hey, that was three years ago." Then a quick look of worry crosses Dinardo's face. "They didn't kill him, did they? Are they back?"

"Why do you think they might have killed him?"

"These were scary guys. Wouldn't surprise me. Keep this between us, huh?"

"No problem," I lie. "I'm bound by attorney-bookmaker confidentiality. What did they look like?"

"I don't remember; it was a long time ago. They were big; one of them had a shaved head, I remember that."

"You don't know their names?"

He shakes his head. "Never did."

"If you see them again, will you call me?" I give him my card.

"Yeah, sure I will," he lies. "But you don't want to know those guys. I don't want to know those guys."

"What are you worried about? You have Rock and last-time guy to protect you."

With nothing else to learn from Jimmy, we head back out. Rock is standing up; he's not gagging anymore and he looks angry.

"That was a sucker punch, asshole," Rock says.

He actually called Marcus an asshole. It is possible that Rock is the dumbest human I have ever encountered, and in my business I run into few Rhodes scholars.

"Let it go, Rock," I say. "Apologize and then let it go."

"Let it go, Rock," last-time guy says.

But Rock doesn't let it go. Once again, he moves threateningly toward Marcus and throws a punch. Marcus moves his head slightly, but enough to let the fist go whizzing by him. Then he comes across with an elbow to Rock's jaw, sending the imbecile down and out for the count.

If you're ever playing a game of Rock, Paper, Marcus . . . go with Marcus.

"I hope Rock can look back on this as a learning experience," I say to last-time guy.

"He seem to you like the kind of guy who learns stuff?"

"Probably not," I say.

"Jimmy pissed that we let you in?"

"I don't think so. Jimmy seems like the understanding type."

We've learned some things, but I wouldn't equate that with making progress.

The good news is that we've gotten some confirmation that Chris was innocent of the original manslaughter charge. With what we heard from the guys in the alley, and Jimmy Dinardo, it is clear that Charlie Burgess lied, and lied for money.

It is also clear that the people who paid him were dangerous and willing to back up their money with violence. There is a strong possibility, close to definite in my mind, that those same people killed Burgess.

It is unlikely that it's a coincidence that just as he contemplated recanting his testimony against Chris, Burgess was killed by someone completely unrelated. It shows how important Burgess's lie was to them then and continues to be now.

We had been operating under the assumption that Chris was telling the truth, so the fact that we now know we were right does not advance the ball much.

We still don't know why Burgess was paid to lie, or more on point, why these people wanted Chris to be put behind bars. Because I don't see anything that Burgess's lie accomplished for anyone other than getting rid of Chris Myers.

So even though we have no idea how to do it, our task is fairly straightforward: we have to find out why dangerous people with money to throw around needed Chris out of the way.

I head down to the jail again to see Chris. We have to rely on him; otherwise we have no chance of figuring out why he was a target. He knows what was going on in his life back then, personal and otherwise. So somewhere in his mind must be the answer.

The team is just sitting around waiting for something to investigate. The only person who can supply it is Chris.

"Did you do your homework?" I ask when he sits down.

He grins. "I did. But I hope you're grading on a curve." He takes a folded piece of paper out of his shirt pocket and hands it to me. "It's everything I remember working on just before I left. But I'm afraid there could be things I'm missing; it's been a while since I thought about that world."

I look at it quickly and then put it in my pocket. "Good. This will be helpful, but keep thinking about it. Maybe something else will pop into your head."

"Did you speak to Vic Everson?"

"I did. He claimed he wanted to be helpful, but couldn't reveal client information."

"He didn't tell you anything?"

"No."

"That's a load of crap. The firm listed clients on their goddamn website. He could tell you plenty without revealing confidences. Some of it is in the public record."

That gives me an idea. "If you had interactions with courts on any of this, it would be public."

"Right. A Nexus search would tell you that."

"What about files within the firm? I assume everything is digitized?"

"Absolutely. But they would have locked me out back then, once I left."

"Maybe we can unlock it."

I leave the jail, and as I'm headed to my car, I call Sam Willis, my vice president in charge of unlocking. As always, he answers on the first ring with "Talk to me." Sam does not share my dim view of phone conversations.

"Sam, there's a New York law firm called Everson, Manning and Winkler."

"Where Chris Myers worked."

"Right. Can you hack into their system?"

"Obviously."

"Sorry, Sam, didn't mean to insult you. I want you to get in and search through Chris's files. I want to know what he was working on when he left, and whatever information about each piece you can find."

"Okay. Any chance he knows what his password was?"

"I don't know. But wouldn't they have cut him out?"

"Maybe not fully; a lot of these companies are surprisingly inept at this stuff. I can get in either way, but the password would help."

"Go see him at the jail and ask. I don't want you to do it over the phone."

"Okay. Let me look at their system first. Maybe it will be easy enough without it. Anything else you need?"

"Yes. The guy that Chris was convicted of killing, Joey Bonaventura. See what you can find out about him."

"Just general background? How deep do you want me to go?"

"As deep as you can."

"You got it, Chief."

Whenever Sam calls me "Chief," it means he's in detective mode.

"Roger, Sergeant Willis."

I asked Sam to dig into Bonaventura because of an idea that's been rattling around in my head. I've been thinking that the Burgess killing might have been blamed on Chris simply because he had the bad luck to be there at the time.

According to this reasoning, he could possibly have just been an unlucky foil in the Bonaventura killing. What if the goal was to remove Bonaventura, and Chris was just someone used to deflect from the real killer? It's not likely . . . it's a long way from that . . . but it's possible.

We're stuck in "anything's possible" mode, which is not a good mode for a defense to be in.

Chris's memory is not exactly photographic.

On the piece of paper he gave me, he starts off by acknowledging that: *Keep in mind that I was badly abusing alcohol at the time. I was in a fog, and I'm afraid that the passage of time doesn't clear it up.* This doesn't bode well for what the rest of his notes might say, but I read on.

Part of the problem, he says, is that he was involved with many cases and clients during his later years at the firm, but many of them would have been concluded by the time Bonaventura was killed. The difficulty is remembering which ones were still active, to say nothing of the details of those cases.

He lists four possibilities, of which the most promising is a case in which the firm was representing a casino in Atlantic City in a dispute over an adjacent piece of property that it wanted to expand onto. The casino had an agreement in principle to buy the land in question, but the owner reneged on the deal.

There does not seem anything sinister about the situation, but since it involves a casino hotel, big money players were involved. Since Burgess's killers were clearly willing to spend money, it makes this scenario a possibility.

Another case is a suit between a small chain of pharmacies in New Jersey and a medium-size drug company. Chris was representing the drug company, which was being sued by the pharmacy chain over the drug company's refusal to continue to do business with them.

The drug company's algorithms had shown that the pharmacy had dispensed far more opioids than would have been normal, and with the increasing pressure on drug companies in this area, they cut the pharmacies off. The drug company did not want to be culpable for lawsuits on the back end, should victims of opioid addiction or their families come after them with lawsuits.

The third case involved a town called Metuska, Pennsylvania. The small town of Metuska was trying to take land from some citizens under eminent domain, saying that it was needed for roads and municipal purposes. Some of those citizens were fighting to keep their property, and they hired Chris's firm. Chris said that religious issues were involved, that the town leaders were suspected of doing these things to aid the local church, and not for needed municipal improvements.

Fourth was a class action suit against the makers of baby carriages that had proven to be defective and had caused injuries to small children. Chris's firm was one of a number of firms pursuing the case on behalf of the plaintiffs. Even among four unlikely causes for the situation Chris is facing, this seems like the least promising.

I call a meeting of the K Team, along with Sam Willis, to discuss how we are going to approach this. I start off by asking Sam if he has gotten anywhere in penetrating Chris's files at Everson, Manning & Winkler.

"Chris did not remember his password, so I went in a different way, but I'm in. That's the good news. The bad news is that Chris worked on a lot of stuff while he was there, and on the face of it it's hard to tell what was still ongoing when he left."

"Err on the side of providing too much," I say. "If something isn't timely or relevant, I'll discard it."

"Well, I think I have it narrowed down to the most recent stuff. Now I have to go through it individually to give you the areas that Chris had an active role in. I'll need another day or two."

"Okay. Obviously the sooner the better. I've made copies for all of you of the page that Chris gave me, detailing what he remembers. It's pretty sketchy, but Sam's work will help fill it in and should give us leads. At the least, it will provide names of people that Chris worked with on each case, and we can follow up with them."

"This covers the work area," Corey says, "but what about the rest of his life? Any relationships gone bad, any important people he might have pissed off? Any nonwork enemies?"

"According to Chris, no. But he was drinking heavily back then, and his memory is not what it could be. We should be checking into whatever we can in that area. I have the names of a couple of people at the firm who were also his friends, and I will be speaking to them about what they know outside Chris's life in the office. But I think the answer is much more likely to be work related."

"I agree," says Corey. "Whatever the reason for getting Chris out of the way, it's obviously still of importance today."

"Not necessarily," Laurie says. "As Andy pointed out to me the other day, they could have killed Burgess simply because they did not want him implicating them by revealing they paid him to lie. The issue itself, the reason for getting Chris out of the way, could have been resolved long ago."

"But let's keep in mind that these people are dangerous," I say. "Whatever their motivation, they have already killed at least once and probably twice to protect themselves; there is no reason to doubt that they would do it again."

Marcus hasn't said a word, which is no great surprise. My guess is he's not thinking, *Well, if Andy told me to be careful, I should be really worried.*

Marcus wasn't born with a "worry gene."

Harold Caruso is one of the people that Chris listed as a friend back in the day. He was also a coworker at the law firm and is still employed there.

Mercifully, Caruso lives in Edgewater, New Jersey, right near the George Washington Bridge, so I don't have to fight city traffic to meet with him. Since it's Saturday, we're getting together at a Starbucks in nearby Fort Lee.

I wait at an inside table for about fifteen minutes until he arrives. He's at least five years older than Chris, maybe more . . . I'm not good at judging age. One thing is for sure: it's been a long time since he's had hair. The top of his head gives off a glare from the overhead lighting.

"Really sorry I'm late. As I was leaving, I got a work call. On a damn weekend, for something that could have easily waited until Monday."

"It's fine. I appreciate your taking the time."

"I have to admit I'm curious about Chris and how he's doing. He was such a good guy, and to see his life spiral like this . . . it's just horrible."

"He's going to be fine." I have no idea if that is true or not.

"Really? I'm glad to hear that."

"You and Chris were friends outside the office?"

"Yes, good friends, going back to college. I'm afraid we

were also drinking buddies." Caruso shakes his head in apparent sadness at the memory. "Instead of helping him through his problems, I probably enabled them by being there every step of the way."

"What kind of problems?"

"Everything stemmed from the drinking, or maybe the drinking stemmed from everything. I don't really know for sure. But his marriage was falling apart, and his work situation was deteriorating. My guess is the alcohol was more the cause than the result."

"Did you ever go to the Basement Bar with him?"

Caruso nods. "I did, maybe three or four times. We used to go to the more upscale bars in the city, but gradually Chris gravitated to the places . . . well, I guess he didn't want to be seen by anyone he worked with.

"The Basement Bar certainly fit that bill, and at first I would go with him. I was even there the night he killed the guy. But I left way before it happened."

"So you still think he killed him in a fight?"

"Yeah, sure. He was convicted of it; I didn't follow the trial that carefully, but I assume there was evidence. And Chris could be volatile when he was drunk; it brought out his temper."

"Were you drunk that night as well?"

Caruso shakes his head. "No, I just had a couple of drinks and left. I didn't like that place . . . it's a total dive. I didn't have the kind of alcohol problem that Chris had. I enjoyed it, but I was never dependent on it. The ironic thing is that I decided after that night that it was enough, that I didn't want to become Chris. So he helped me without knowing it."

"Did you know Bonaventura, the guy who was killed?"

"No. I don't know anything about him."

"What about Charlie Burgess?"

"That's the guy Chris killed . . . is accused of killing?"

"Yes."

"No. I mean maybe I saw him or met him at the bar, but I have no recollection of it. Chris and I weren't really there to socialize."

"Let's say, just for the sake of argument, that someone wanted Chris out of the way back then."

"Out of the way, like in jail?" I can hear the skepticism in Caruso's voice already.

"Like in jail, or just out of the way. Could that have been related to his job?"

"You mean, would the firm want him gone? They fired him after the trouble started, and they could have done that anytime; why would they want him in jail? I'm sorry, but that's ridiculous."

"Not necessarily the firm. I wouldn't limit it to that. I would include his clients, adversaries in the cases, anyone at all involved."

"It doesn't seem possible, or at least I'm not aware of any such thing. I never heard Chris express any worry about anything like that, or any suspicions."

"Was he functioning in his job, or was the alcohol interfering?"

Caruso is quiet for a few moments, as if weighing his words. He could be deciding whether to be careful, or truthful. "Chris was a terrific attorney. A real asset to the firm."

"Until the end?"

"No, I'm afraid not. The drinking, and the trouble

at home, was taking its toll. Chris would come in late, leave early, and work stuff would slip through the cracks. He made some mistakes that were not typical for the old Chris, and which were frankly unacceptable for a lawyer of his experience and talent. I worked right next to him, so I covered for him a lot."

"Who took on Chris's clients when he left? Everson wouldn't tell me."

"He wouldn't? That's strange. Anyway, you're looking at him. I wound up with most of it. But there wasn't that much; Vic Everson had cut back on Chris's assignments because of his performance."

"And there was nothing in any of those cases that could have brought this on? That could have had dangerous people wanting him out of the picture?"

Caruso shakes his head. "No, certainly not that I remember. You need to understand that at the end, Vic knew enough not to give him crucial work. Vic kept him on way longer than he probably should have. But the stuff I inherited was not that significant, for various reasons."

"Can I come to you if I have any questions about it?"

"Sure. I mean, even though it's a while back, there could be confidentiality issues, which I'm sure you understand. But I'll help however I can."

"Thanks."

"Can you get Chris off?"

I evade the question slightly. "Well, he did not kill Charlie Burgess or Joey Bonaventura."

"Whoa . . . I didn't expect that. Do you know who did kill them?"

"Not yet, but we're getting there."

When I get back from the morning walk with Tara, Sebastian, and Hunter, I am surprised that Corey and Simon Garfunkel are at the house.

Tara is delighted, her tail goes into full-wag mode when she sees Simon. They are best friends and in the same age bracket, so they wrestle gently with each other.

Corey is in the kitchen chomping down on Laurie's pancakes. Laurie is not the greatest cook in the world, but her pancakes take a back seat to no one's.

There is one problem here . . . it's the elephant pancake in the room. The particular pancakes that Corey is inhaling were meant for me. That would not be such a big deal if, when I walked into the kitchen, Laurie hadn't held up the empty pitcher of pancake batter and given a shrug indicating that she's all out.

I decide to tackle this head-on. "You're eating my pancakes." I am at my most confrontational at breakfast.

Corey smiles, though it's hard for him to talk with his mouth so full. "Thanks, they're great," he mumbles.

"Corey says he has something significant to tell us," Laurie says.

"Did he tell you what it is? Or did he just sit down and

start chomping?" If what I just said embarrasses Corey, he's not showing it.

She shakes her head. "He was about to, and then he saw the pancakes."

We wait patiently for Corey to finish, although he's chewing so fast that it doesn't take long. Finally he pushes himself away from the table and turns to me. "Wow, you don't know what you just missed."

"Actually, I do. The only thing that could make up for that performance is for you to tell me the name of the real murderer, along with proof to present to the jury."

"I can't quite go that far, but what I have is pretty good. Do you know who Chris's wife, Jessica, started dating after she left Chris?"

"I don't."

"None other than Paul Donnelly Jr."

"Wow" is all I can get out in the moment. Paul Donnelly Jr.'s father, cleverly named Paul Donnelly Sr., has long been a leading figure in organized crime in the Bronx. Both men were in the news about four months ago, as there was a drive-by shooting that was said to target Paul Sr. outside a restaurant on Central Park Avenue in Yonkers.

Senior was uninjured in the attack, but there was one fatality, someone who was not thought to be a target.

Paul Donnelly Jr.

Corey has no more information yet beyond this bombshell; he decided correctly that we needed to know this immediately, or at least right after he finished his pancakes. My pancakes.

Even though I'm still hungry, I head down to the jail to

talk to my client. When he's brought in, I get right to it; I'm not in the mood for small talk.

"Why didn't you tell me who Jessica's boyfriend was?"

"You mean Donnelly?"

"You know damn well I mean Donnelly."

"Because Jessica has nothing to do with this. Donnelly was a longtime friend of both of ours; we all went to college together. His relationship with Jessica came afterwards; I even spoke to him about it a few times and told him I was fine with it. Paul made a great living in jewelry; he had established himself. And he was prominent in the art world; he wasn't in Daddy's business."

"I asked you if there was anything in your personal life that I should know, anything that might have connected you to dangerous people. Your wife was with a crime boss's son after you, and you didn't think that was worth mentioning?"

"You're right. I'm sorry. I guess I was subconsciously trying to protect Jessica, and I really don't think—"

I interrupt, still pretty angry. "I'm going to tell you this as clearly as I can. If you want me to represent you, you will play by my rules. You will withhold nothing that could even be remotely relevant, and you'll let me make the decisions about what is important and what isn't. Or you can get another lawyer."

"I hear you."

"Do you still have a relationship with Jessica?"

He nods. "We're fine. Or at least we were before this happened. I haven't talked to her since I was arrested again."

"Good. I want to talk to her. Set it up."

"Okay."

"Let me know when you do."

I leave Chris to do that. I was tough on him, but in a situation like this I have to be. We need every piece of information we can get our hands on, and we simply cannot have our own client withholding any, even if he isn't doing it deliberately.

Sam Willis calls. "I've also got some information on Bonaventura; I should have it locked down by tomorrow. Can I come over in the morning?"

"You looking for some pancakes? Is that what this is about?"

"It had entered my mind."

"I'll ask Laurie to make extra."

"A lot extra."

By the time Sam is finished eating, we are going to be selecting a jury.

It's not that he eats slowly, it's more a quantity thing. Fortunately, Laurie has compensated and made extra pancake batter, so there should be a couple left for me.

When he's finally finished, he turns to the matter at hand. "So I've checked into Joey Bonaventura."

"And?"

Sam dispenses information slowly; he seems to like the spotlight and the drama of the moment. Unfortunately, I've already used up most of my patience as a result of the Corey Douglas pancake incident yesterday.

"And he moved here from Louisville about a month before he died. He worked down there as a computer consultant, so I assume he did the same thing here, but there is no evidence of it that I can find.

"He wasn't married and had less than three thousand dollars in the bank."

"So far this is less than fascinating, Sam."

Laurie seems frustrated as well, but she's way too nice to say anything.

"It gets better," Sam says.

"Good. Does it also get faster?"

"I think it's fake. The entire identity . . . I think it's fake."

"Why?"

"Because it's all on the surface. If you dig deep, there's nothing there, and what is there probably isn't true."

"Give me an example."

"I can't find him anywhere in Louisville. No house, no rental, nothing. Now it's possible he stayed with a friend, but he also did not have a Kentucky driver's license."

"Where did he stay when he moved up here?"

"Allegedly a motel in Paramus. There is a record of him there, including an advance payment in cash. Which is suspicious in itself."

"Next of kin?"

"I can't find any; maybe the police did."

"A guy with less than three thousand dollars in the bank pays for a motel for a month in advance? With cash?" I ask.

"I don't buy it," Sam says.

"Did he have credit cards?"

"Not a one. I'm still searching. Wouldn't the police have dug into this?"

"Not necessarily," Laurie says. "He was the victim, not a potential perpetrator. They would just have looked on the surface, made an attempt to find someone to notify, but wouldn't have been that aggressive when the search turned up empty."

"Seems strange," Sam says.

She nods. "It was a guy in a fight in a dark alley behind a crummy bar, not a congressman at the Four Seasons. It shouldn't be the case, but different victims and situations provoke different levels of interest."

We send Sam off to keep digging into Bonaventura,

while I talk about the impact of this information with Laurie.

"This feels like a big deal," Laurie says. "If Bonaventura was not who he seemed to be, there has to be a reason."

"True, but he could have been on the run or concealing his real identity, having nothing to do with Chris. Maybe he was evading the police."

"Unlikely. His DNA would have been on file if he had ever been arrested. The police would have run it when he turned up dead."

"So maybe he wasn't Joey Bonaventura, but he was someone. Or maybe he was Bonaventura, but had made an effort to conceal his real background. You can fake an identity, and a history, but not a dead body. The good news is that it gives us another avenue to pursue . . . finding out who the hell this guy was."

"Is there bad news?" she asks.

"Always is. This time it's yet another example that the people we're up against are smart. They're not just one step ahead of us; it feels like they've taken steps we aren't close to finding out about yet.

"The first thing we have to learn is whether the police put his DNA into the national database. If so, maybe they got a hit on Joey Bonaventura and Sam is off base with his theory. If they didn't get a hit, we're back where we started. And if they didn't run it, we need to get them to do so."

"Right," Laurie says.

"Can you take care of that?" This is an example of a time when Laurie's relationship with the Paterson police comes in handy; she knows a lot of the players who can make this happen.

"I think so."

"Let me know if you run into a brick wall, or if they are just slow to move, and I'll ask the judge to issue an order. I think she'll do it, but I'd rather not tip our hand to the prosecution as to which way we are headed."

"Will do," she says. "What are we hoping for?"

"That they never ran it at all. Because then we can get it done and maybe find out who the hell this guy was."

What I don't bother saying, but which I'm starting to consider, is the increasing possibility that this wasn't about Chris at all, that it was about whoever the victim turns out to have been.

Under this theory, Chris was just in the wrong place at the wrong time and was more vulnerable because of his drinking. That would also mean that analyzing his cases, and his wife's relationship with her mob-connected boyfriend, are by definition dead ends.

Burgess would still have been killed to keep quiet about who paid him to lie, but the reason they paid him was not to put Chris away, but rather to shield the real killers from further investigation.

I'm not sure which scenario I'm hoping for because so far we are nowhere in either case.

So we'll know when we know.

The first thing about Jessica Myers that surprises me is that she didn't revert to her maiden name after the divorce.

I don't know why she chose that, but it earns her a point in the Andy Carpenter merit system. Many women whose ex-husbands were in jail for manslaughter would be ashamed and embarrassed and would try to distance themselves. Apparently not Jessica Myers.

The other thing about her that surprises me is her looks. She is drop-dead beautiful . . . almost in Laurie's class. Trust me, that is a small class. I don't know why I'm surprised by this, but I am.

Jessica lives in Montclair. Her house is a large colonial in an obviously upscale neighborhood; Chris told me it was their house when they divorced, and she got it in the settlement.

She greets me at the door with a welcoming smile and a mastiff by her side. I'm particularly partial to mastiffs, and this one is large and spectacular. Looks-wise, he is the Jessica Myers of mastiffs.

"Andy?"

Since that's actually my name, I say, "Yes." I have always been a gifted conversationalist with women.

"Come in."

She leads me into the den. The house is obviously expensively furnished. Some pieces of art on the walls must be worth a lot of money, or maybe they're worth zero . . . I have no idea. I know as much about art as I do about microbiology, Buddhism, and women, which is to say, nothing.

We sit in the den, or at least I do. She goes off somewhere and comes back with coffee and cookies. "I hope you drink regular coffee?"

"Regularly. You have a beautiful house." Clearly I'm on a conversational roll.

"Thank you. Please tell me Chris is going to be okay."

"I believe that he will, and I'm hoping you can help."

"How?"

"Chris didn't commit either crime, that I know for certain."

She takes a deep breath. "I'm relieved but not surprised to hear that."

I nod. "I was relieved to find it out myself."

"You still haven't told me how I can help," she points out accurately.

I'm still not sure how to broach this. Broaching has never been a specialty of mine. Laurie is my vice president in charge of broaching, but she's not here.

"We're trying to focus on finding people who back then had an interest in removing Chris from the life he was living, either in his work or his personal life. Putting him in prison accomplished that goal."

"I certainly never wanted to hurt him."

"I know that. Trust me, you're not a suspect. The person I wanted to talk to you about is Paul Donnelly Jr."

She looks surprised and somewhat wary. "Paul? I don't understand."

"It's possible, or at least worth our checking out, whether when he started in a relationship with you, he considered Chris, as your ex-husband, a threat to that relationship."

"What would . . . ?" Then she nods her understanding. That brings with it a frown. "I hope you're not counting too hard on this theory."

"No, it's just one of a number of theories we have, but we have to examine each one."

"Well, this one is a waste of your time. For many reasons."

"What are they?"

"For one thing, Paul and I broke up shortly before he . . . died."

I don't bother pointing out that this is beside the point, since we are talking about a time when they were together. Instead I let her continue.

"For another, Paul had nothing to do with his father's . . . business. He loved his father, but hated and was ashamed of what he did. Shall I continue?"

"Please."

"Paul was Chris's friend, and my friend, long before I entered into a relationship with him. We all went to Ohio State together, Paul and Chris and me and Harold Caruso and a few others. That friendship lasted for a very long time; in some cases it still lasts today.

"Paul was as gentle and caring a man as anyone I ever

met. Not only was he an expert on fine gems, and that became his career, but he was also a lover of art and opera. He was even a wonderful painter himself.

"He did not have a mean bone in his body. We just weren't right for each other, for reasons having nothing to do with his father. Paul could not have killed or framed anyone; and he had absolutely no jealousy or concern about Chris. That's not close to the person who Paul was.

"And lastly, Paul is dead. All he did was go out to dinner with his father that night, and he died because of it. It was devastating to me; even though we had just ended our relationship, we remained close friends, and I suspect would have stayed that way.

"But as I understand it, this latest crime that Chris is accused of happened long after Paul's death. How could Paul or his father have been responsible for that?"

The question is answerable. It's unlikely Paul would have dirtied his hands and done things directly; it's more likely that he would have gone to his father and had the killing and framing done. Those people would still have wanted to remove Burgess from the picture, so that he could not expose them.

I don't tell her any of that because it wouldn't be productive. I ask instead, "Have you ever met Paul Sr.?"

"Oh, yes. A few times we went out to dinner; Paul's mother was usually there as well. The other time we went to a family function, a wedding. I know who Paul's father is in real life, and what he does, but he could not have been more gracious to me. He still keeps in touch with me; he's very protective."

I'm not going to get any more out of Jessica beyond

maybe another cup of coffee and a few cookies. I'm sure she's being honest in believing that there is no way Paul Donnelly Jr., or Sr., had anything to with our case.

But that doesn't mean she's right.

I am not ready to eliminate the Paul Donnelly connection as the source of Chris's troubles.

Someone like Paul Donnelly Sr. would have had the resources, the means, the willingness to commit violence, and the lack of conscience necessary to murder. People with all those qualifications are few and far between. Defense lawyers like me cherish them.

That Donnelly Sr. obviously likes Jessica, is protective of her, and keeps in touch with her even with his son dead, increases my interest in him.

Another reason I'm hanging on to this theory is that I don't have any other viable ones, at least not yet. We defense strategists abhor a vacuum, so until I have something to displace him, I'm keeping Donnelly Sr. on the front burner.

On the evening walk with the dogs, I run the theory past Tara. There is no chance she knows what the hell I'm talking about, but golden retrievers are excellent sounding boards. They're smart and empathetic, and the fact that they don't talk prevents them from telling the speaking human that he or she is an idiot, no matter how stupid the person sounds.

Goldens would make great shrinks.

Sam had called to tell me that he has updates on his projects for me. I tell him we'll meet at the office in the morning. Since I have the office, I might as well start using it, but Ricky is the main reason I'd rather not do all of the legal work at our house.

Ricky is only twelve years old, so I don't want him to overhear so much talk about murders. It can't be good for his emotional development. I want him to be secure in the safety of his room, playing video games in which he kills and maims thousands of virtual people in one sitting.

I don't expect praise . . . this kind of consideration is just what caring parents do.

But I don't need to go to the office to get updates from Laurie, and when I get home, she has one for me: "Donnie Jacobs got me the DNA information on Bonaventura."

"That was fast." Laurie's relationships and personality get things like this done in a hurry. If I had tried it, the information would have come to me around the time of the next lunar eclipse.

"Yeah, Donnie's a good guy. Stayed late to check the files, which were in storage."

"Had they run Bonaventura's . . . or whoever's . . . DNA?"

She nods. "Yes. And it turned up nothing; it was not in any of the databases."

"That means he was never arrested and probably never served in the military."

Laurie knows that as well as I do. "So where does that leave us?"

"Basically nowhere, when it comes to Bonaventura. And we're already nowhere when it comes to everything else."

"What about the private DNA services, the ones people send their DNA to in order to learn about their ancestors, or maybe current relatives that they didn't know about? I bet that wasn't checked by the cops."

"I would have to get a court order," I say.

"Can you?"

"It's worth a shot. In the meantime, I want to get the discovery from the Bonaventura case. We haven't gotten it because that's not the case we're trying. But I think I can get the judge to okay it."

I call Eddie Dowd and tell him that I need briefs filed to get the Bonaventura discovery documents and to request that Judge McVay issue an order allowing us to get DNA information from the private services.

The first request should be easy; Burgess clearly has a connection to the Bonaventura case, and there would be no harm in our receiving that information.

The second one is likely to be more problematic. Eddie is going to write it fairly vaguely and mostly describe our need to connect with people who knew Bonaventura, so we can learn things like whether he and Burgess had a prior connection, something that might have given Burgess a reason to lie.

One thing I don't want is for the prosecution to find out that we have doubts as to whether the victim was really someone named Joey Bonaventura at all. I don't want them investigating on their own, or trying to anticipate and damage our defense strategy.

Of course, if Bonaventura is real and he sold vacuum cleaners in Louisville before coming to New Jersey to study in a seminary, then I'd be fine with the prosecution wasting its time.

But like everything else, it remains to be seen.

My office consists of three fairly pathetic rooms above a fruit stand on Van Houten Street in Paterson. I've had it since the day I opened my practice, when I had so little money that I could barely pay the rent.

Sofia Hernandez owns the fruit stand and is my landlord. I'm wealthy now and obviously could move into nicer offices, but I stay here for three reasons. One is that moving to new offices makes a statement that I am going to be working for a long time; I'm not ready to go out on that employment limb.

Another is that I like Sofia and it would disappoint her if I left. But the main reason I'm attached to this place is that it takes me back to my roots, figuratively and even literally in that Sofia's stand has an entire wall of root vegetables.

Sam Willis, who also functions as my accountant when he isn't pretending to be Dick Tracy, has an office down the hall from me. His is tiny; it makes mine look like Madison Square Garden.

Sam obviously hears me come up the steps to my office since he appears within seconds after I arrive. He's carrying a bag and I ask what it is.

"I figured you might want some doughnuts."

On the food chain, Sam occupies a spot on the "taking"

link, not the "giving" one, so I'm surprised that he's bringing doughnuts. Surprised and suspicious.

"What kind did you get?"

"Vanilla-crème filled, a half dozen. Your favorite."

Uh-oh. Sam wants something. He wouldn't spring for a half dozen vanilla-crème filled doughnuts unless he had an angle. But there's no sense in my asking him what it is because knowing Sam, it will come out at its own pace. And I'm not that anxious to hear it.

So instead I ask him to start telling me what he's learned, while I begin stuffing doughnuts into my face. The trick to eating a crème or jelly doughnut is to make the first bite into the hole on the outside; that way no filling escapes and makes a mess. It's a complicated procedure, but with a great deal of practice I've become quite proficient at it.

"So I found a few interesting things. Especially as it relates to the issue with the pharmacies dispensing large supplies of opioids."

Sam is referring to a case that Chris worked on at the law firm. RX and More, a small chain of pharmacies, was suing Harkin Pharmaceuticals because the company had ended their relationship and wouldn't supply RX and More with prescription drugs. Harkin's algorithms had found that RX and More was dispensing far more than would have been considered normal.

"What about it?"

"Well, it turns out that the lawsuit never came close to a courtroom, or a settlement, because the Feds busted RX and More. Harkin was right; RX and More was creating fake prescriptions and then filling them. The drugs were winding up on the street."

This is interesting; if drugs and drug dealers were involved, then violence could easily be suspected. "So who got busted? The company, or individuals?"

"The company didn't face criminal liability. But they paid a big fine, and they were basically forced to sell out to a bigger chain."

"How many stores did RX and More have?"

"Thirty-seven, in New Jersey, New York, Connecticut, and Massachusetts. And while the company was not held criminally liable, two executives were arrested and took plea bargains. They're serving time now."

"I know Chris represented the drug company, but is there anything you've seen that would have made him any kind of target?"

"Not directly, but I haven't gotten to the good part yet. The other person arrested and convicted in this case, but who was not working for RX and More, was a guy name Anthony 'the Whale' Fusco."

I like what I'm hearing so far; Anthony "the Whale" Fusco sounds like he could be involved with the kind of people I'm interested in. If you get a nickname like the Whale, you're probably not a librarian, or a guy that a girl would bring home to meet her parents: *Mom, Dad . . . I'd like you to meet my fiancé, Anthony "the Whale" Fusco.*

"Tell me about the Whale."

"He went down for selling and distributing the opioids. Wouldn't rat on anyone . . . said he was operating on his own. That seems unlikely to me, but that's not really my area. But get this, there are media reports linking him to the Paul Donnelly crime family."

So twice the senior Donnelly's name has come up in

connection to Chris. Once because is son had a relationship with Jessica Myers, Chris's ex-wife, and now this. I don't know how the two issues connect, but we need to figure it out because I don't believe this is a coincidence.

"Okay, Sam, you're two for two . . . keep going."

"Two? I only told you about one thing so far."

"I was including the doughnuts."

Sam nods. "I thought you'd like that. Let's move on to Atlantic City. Carlyle Equity Partners, a private financial company based in New York, has a portfolio that includes a lot of casino investments. One of their hotels in Atlantic City wanted to expand, and to do so they needed a piece of property near them. It included a strip mall and a few apartments.

"The owner first agreed to sell and then backed out. He said Carlyle changed the terms of the agreement, which the company disputed. Chris's firm represented Carlyle, and Chris worked on the case.

"But here's the interesting part. Before the case could come to a conclusion, the owner, a guy named Steven Ivey, was killed in a hit-and-run accident. The driver was never found, and Ivey's estate then sold the property to Carlyle."

This is a little less interesting than the Donnelly drug case because it doesn't include Donnelly, and I can't see why getting Chris out of the way would have benefited either party. But I'm not going to dismiss it out of hand. "Okay, worth pursuing. Anything else, Sam?"

"One more thing, which I really want to talk to you about."

Uh-oh . . . here it comes. In this business, there's no such thing as a free doughnut.

"There's a small town in Pennsylvania called Metuska; it has less than four thousand people in it. Used to be larger, there was a plant that made hand tools, but that went under. After a while it was taken over by some religious sect; they make religious ornaments of some kind."

"So?"

"So for some reason, and I'm not sure why yet, the local government started trying to take land that people owned, a lot of it being the lots that held their residences. They were using eminent domain. As best as I can tell, it seems like some of the people were fine with that; they were paying good prices, and the town wasn't exactly thriving anyway, so they were happy to leave."

"Where does Chris come in?" I ask, trying to move this saga along.

"I'm getting there. One of the citizens organized some kind of group to fight the eminent domain legally. His name is Alex Swain. He collected money from the other residents to pay for lawyers and legal fees. That's where Chris comes in; Swain hired Chris's firm."

"And they must have assigned Chris."

"Seems so. Anyway, the whole thing fell apart when Swain took off with the money. There's a bunch of stuff about it on social media from some of the people he swindled; they also found out that he sold his house before leaving."

"Do we know where Swain is now?"

Sam shakes his head. "No. I did a basic search on him, but he did not turn up. He must be using a different identity; maybe he's afraid that the people he swindled called the cops."

"Okay, thanks, Sam."

"I wanted to ask you a favor, Andy."

Here it comes. "What's that, Sam?"

"Let me go to Metuska and check it out."

"Check what out?"

"You know, get the lay of the land."

"You want to get the lay of the land? In Metuska, Pennsylvania?"

"Yeah, I can figure out whether this has anything to do with the case. There's nothing like being on the ground; that's where you get a feel for things."

I'm not seeing any big harm in this. Sam has longed to play detective and get in on what he considers the "action." One time it almost got him killed. But in this case, there would seem to be little harm for him to do; I don't think the answer to the two murders in Paterson, New Jersey, has anything to do with Metuska, Pennsylvania.

Also, regardless of whether this is meaningful for us, we need to check everything out, and Sam can do that. Well, maybe he can do that. Actually, I doubt if he can do that, but he can try.

So I suppose I can say fine and let him go have fun. I mean, the guy did buy me crème-filled doughnuts.

"Sam, I need you here doing your cyber stuff for us. You're indispensable."

"I can do it from there, Andy. I can do it from anywhere. Just need a computer and an internet connection. I'll bring my computer, and I'm sure Metuska can get me online."

"There's one other thing. You absolutely cannot shoot anyone, no matter what. That's a rule."

"What about a Taser?"

"Sam . . ."

"I'm just joking, Andy. No shooting anyone, with anything. I'll leave right away."

"Okay, go spend Christmas in Metuska, on me."

t's frustrating that Chris can give us so little information about his own life.

Unfortunately, he spent the time we are concerned with in something of an alcohol-induced haze. I'm sure it's just as frustrating for him as it is for us, even more so, since it's his life that is on the line.

I'm back at the jail to talk to him about it again. My hope is that as I learn things, discussing them with Chris will jog his memory and cut through the haze.

Our conversation starts the same way almost every conversation I've ever had with people in his position starts. He asks about progress in the case, and I trot out my patented "We're getting there, but we have a long way to go." This time I throw in, "And we can use your help."

"How?"

"To fill in more of the blanks on some of your work stuff."

He frowns his frustration. "Believe me, Andy, I'm trying. You have no idea how hard I'm trying."

"I can imagine. Were you able to function in those days? I mean, at work?"

"Yes, I actually did a pretty good job of not letting

the drinking get in the way of work. There were problems. . . . I overslept some times, and a few things fell through the cracks. But I think I did my job reasonably well. It's just that the drinking left my memory of those days pretty thin."

"Let's talk about the RX and More case. Your clients were being sued by RX and More pharmacies because they had refused to do business with them. Harkin said that RX and More was filling way too many opioid prescriptions, well beyond normal."

"Right," he says a little shakily.

"Do you know how the case resolved itself after you left?"

"I have no idea; I was in jail, and that was the last thing on my mind."

"The case was dropped because the Feds came in and exposed what RX and More was doing. Two of their executives, and an outside contact, all went to jail for distribution of illegal narcotics."

"Wow . . . didn't know that."

"Did you ever hear of a person named Anthony 'the Whale' Fusco"?

"Seriously?"

"Seriously. He's the outside guy who went to jail."

Chris shakes his head. "I don't think I ever heard of him. That name I would probably remember."

"Did you know that Paul Donnelly was involved? The Whale worked for him."

Chris looks surprised. "No. You don't mean Jessica's boyfriend, right? You mean Paul Sr."

"Right. Paul Sr."

"No, I was unaware of that. Or at least I think I was. Andy,

I didn't even know that RX and More was an organized-crime situation. I remember RX and More gave us data that said Harkin was making a mistake. But I didn't buy it; I thought we were on the right side of this. And we were."

"Let's talk about the Atlantic City casino thing. Does the name Steven Ivey ring a bell?"

Chris thinks for a few moments. "I think so. Was he the guy who reneged on the deal to sell his property? He's the guy we were suing, right?"

"Right. Do you know how that wound up?"

"Sorry, no."

"The lawsuit never went forward. Ivey died in a hit-and-run accident, and his estate sold the property."

"Please don't tell me Paul Donnelly was involved with that."

"I don't know one way or the other, but I have no indication that he was. The driver was never found."

"It was a fairly straightforward contract dispute, Andy. And if I remember correctly, and I admit that's a long shot in my situation, but I think we were definitely going to prevail on the merits. We had a very strong case; the guy reneged on a signed deal."

"So no need to get rid of Steven Ivey?"

"Certainly none that I know of. Carlyle would have gotten the land one way or the other; it just might have taken a few months."

"Okay, now let's head down memory lane to Metuska, Pennsylvania. Did you ever actually go there?"

"Yes; it's a really small town with absolutely nothing going on. Makes Mayberry look like Vegas. I was there for maybe an hour, just to get the lay of the land."

Sam is also intent on learning the lay of the land in Metuska; maybe I should just have had him talk to Chris. It could have saved Sam a trip.

"Who was your client?"

"A group of the townspeople. The local government was trying to displace a bunch of them through eminent domain. They were fighting it, although I'm not sure why. If I was them, I would have loved to get out of there."

"Why?"

"Just a depressing place. And there was some kind of religious thing going on there; the mayor and the guy who owned the factory in town, they belonged to some strange religion I had never heard of."

"Was your client Alex Swain?"

"Yeah, I'm pretty sure that was his name. I don't think I actually met him; he was away or something when I was there. I just don't remember him at all."

"Did you have a strong case?"

"I'm not sure. I remember I was planning to try and get the state government to take a look at it. Even though local governments can invoke eminent domain, they can be overruled. It didn't seem right that this dinky little government should be able to displace those people without due process."

"Did you know that Swain secretly sold his house and took off with the townspeople's money?"

"He did?"

"Yes. I have one of my top investigators looking into it now. And he promised not to shoot anybody."

Chris has no idea what I'm talking about, nor should he. "Those people trusted him. Actually, I just remembered something, someone I spoke to. Her name was Hellman . . . or Holman . . . something like that. Swain was away, and she showed me around. Nice lady. I think she was a fourth-grade teacher, though I definitely could have the grade wrong. How did the case wind up?"

"It went nowhere, probably because they didn't have the money to pursue it after Swain swindled them. I assume the town got what they wanted, but I don't know that for sure."

"Terrible that he would do that."

I certainly don't disagree with that. Maybe I should tell Sam that if he runs into Swain, it's okay to shoot just him.

I once again tell Chris to try to think more about those days. He did fill in a few details this time, so we're making some progress.

Very slow, very small progress.

like Christmas, but I have some problems with the Christmas season.

It goes on too long, even out there in the real world. But Laurie's version lasts four months, which means Christmas music in the house from Halloween to the end of February. There is a limit to how much Bing Crosby and Nat King Cole a human should have to take.

So the parts of the season that I like include cold weather, snow, gift giving, colored lights on houses, not working, no mosquitoes, and *Die Hard*. I also like that it's in the middle of football bowl season, and the NFL playoffs are on the horizon. I like that people don't talk insufferably about their golf games. All of that is good.

I don't like the music, the gooey TV shows and movies, gift receiving, and the poignant reality that the NFL season will soon be over. I don't like grown-ups talking about Santa, and newscasters pretending that they are tracking his sleigh.

So all in all, Christmas is a net plus, but I don't count off days on a calendar until it gets here.

Laurie likes us all to open our gifts on Christmas morning, so we're doing that. I did pretty well on the gift-buying front this year. On our behalf Laurie bought Ricky a new video console and some games, as well as a tennis racket, since Sebastian took a bite out of his old racket. It was a metal racket, but that didn't deter Sebastian. There is nothing that dog won't eat.

As for Laurie, I had no idea what to get her, so I asked, "What would you like me to surprise you with this year?"

Since it's the same question I ask every year, she was ready with an answer. "I would love to be surprised by a new exercise bike. And if not that, then I'd love to be surprised by an Apple Watch."

So it worked out great. I ordered the bike online, but I went to the Apple Store in Paramus to get the watch. It was a madhouse; more people were in that store than at the average Jets game. But the staff were efficient, and I walked out of there twenty minutes later with the watch.

I put it under the tree, as instructed, and I told her that the bike would be delivered tomorrow. When she opened the watch, she pretended to almost fall over in shock and surprise.

I have survived another gift-giving season.

On the gift-receiving front, I got shirts from Laurie and more shirts from Ricky. I wasn't as surprised as Laurie, since I told her I needed shirts.

Then I settled in to enjoy the three best things Christmas Day has to offer . . . time with the family, human and canine, watching five excellent NBA basketball games, and eating the terrific holiday dinner that Laurie always makes.

She apparently confuses Christmas with Thanksgiving and always makes turkey, stuffing, yams, et cetera. Since

I like that stuff a lot, I don't point out that she seems to have her holidays mixed up.

The only negative part of the day is that, try as I might, I can't block the case from my mind. The trial will be on us before we know it; it always is.

The evidence and motive against Chris is not faked or planted or made up. He did have reason to hate Burgess, Chris was on the scene, and he did run off after the shooting. We are not going to be able to refute any of that because it's real.

So while we might cast doubt on the meaning of each individual piece, we are going to have to suggest possible alternative killers, to instill reasonable doubt.

At the top of our short list right now is Paul Donnelly Sr. He is connected to Chris in two ways, through his now-deceased son's relationship with Jessica Myers, and through the opioid case, which resulted in his man Tony the Whale Fusco going down along with two RX and More executives.

Few people, probably not even Kevin Bacon, have connections to an organized crime kingpin, and Chris had two of them. This has to make Donnelly Suspect Number One for us. Unfortunately, the roles of Suspect Number Two and Suspect Number Three have not been cast yet.

I call Corey Douglas and ask him to find me someone to talk to who can help me understand if Donnelly is a viable suspect. Corey and Laurie, as ex-cops, are tied into an unofficial network that can reach any law enforcement officer anywhere, so I give Laurie the same assignment.

Corey is the type who doesn't mind that I am bothering him on Christmas, and Laurie is also fine with it, possibly because of the exercise bike and the Apple Watch.

Having set that in motion, I take the dogs for their evening walk. Sebastian hasn't had a tennis racket to eat in a while, so I need to be careful not to walk him near any parked cars. Eating a Volkswagen could upset his stomach.

When we get home, I settle in to watch the final two NBA games of the day. I'll be asleep by halftime of the last one, since it starts at ten thirty. But that's okay; Phoenix at Utah doesn't really do it for me.

All in all, it's been a good Christmas Day. Too bad the season in our house is nowhere near over.

Around here, Bing and Nat are just getting started.

Corey found me an expert on everything Paul Donnelly, but he's not a cop.

Brian Bowers used to be a cop, but retired not long ago. Now he teaches criminology at Bronx Community College, and he's agreed to see me in his office.

The campus is an oasis of green in the cement world that is the Bronx. It's near Jerome Avenue, but far enough away to make it impossible to hear the rumbling sound of the elevated subway. There is a nice quad area, and right now there would be students out throwing Frisbees if it weren't Christmas break and fifteen degrees and everything weren't covered in snow and ice.

This used to be what they called the University Heights campus of NYU. It's thirteen miles and a hundred light-years from the main NYU campus in Greenwich Village.

Bowers has an office in Loew Hall, and he's arriving at the same time that I am. I can tell it's him because when he sees me, he asks, "Andy Carpenter?"

"Guilty as charged."

He smiles and invites me in. We head up to his office on the second floor. I always picture college professors' offices as incredibly cluttered, with papers and books lying around in an order only understandable to that particular professor.

Not in this case. Bowers's office is neat as a pin; papers are in folders and books are on bookshelves. I haven't looked, but they're probably in alphabetical order by author. This guy is still more cop than professor.

"So how's retirement?" I'm afraid that he'll tell me I don't know what I'm missing.

"Mixed. I miss the action, and I love not being in the action. I miss the pressure, and I love not being under pressure." He laughs. "It's only been six months, so let's just say I'm a work in progress."

"A shrink would say that it's good you're in touch with your feelings."

Another smile. "That doesn't make me feel that much better. So how do you know Corey?"

"He's my wife's partner in an investigative team."

Bowers nods. "We worked together once on an interstate case. Does he still have Simon Garfunkel? I was afraid to ask him when he called."

"Oh, yes. Simon is going strong."

"Great dog." Then we move right to business. "Corey said you wanted to talk about Paul Donnelly."

"And he said you were an expert on the subject."

Bowers frowns. "I'm afraid not. I chased him for a lot of years and always came up empty. He was my white whale."

"Tony 'the Whale' Fusco wasn't your whale?"

"I know Tony quite well also."

"How big is he?"

Bowers laughs. "He's not called the Whale because he's

big. He was a big, and very bad, bettor on sports. Actually, he'd bet on anything. He was in deep to Donnelly, so he switched sides and started working for him."

"And wound up in jail for the opioid situation."

"Right. He was just following Donnelly's orders and took the fall in his place."

"Why did he do that?"

"Because he wanted to be alive in jail rather than dead on the outside. And I'm sure Donnelly is taking care of his family quite well." Then, "So how can I help?"

"Donnelly's name has come up twice in a case I'm working on, and I'm trying to figure out if it's meaningful. The first one was the opioid case. My client was an attorney representing Harkin Pharmaceuticals."

"Did he piss Donnelly off in any way?"

"Not that I know of, and not that he knows of. But his memory is a bit shaky."

"What was the other connection?"

"Donnelly's son was in a relationship with my client's ex-wife. It started soon after they divorced. She says that Donnelly Sr. took a liking to her and still is protective of her."

"So what do you think Donnelly might have done to your client?"

"My client was wrongly convicted of involuntary manslaughter because of a person who was paid to lie."

Bowers frowns slightly, and I might even detect a small eye roll. When a cop, or an ex-cop, hears "wrongly convicted," he tends to be skeptical.

"Just take it as fact for the purpose of this conversation, okay? The witness was prepared to recant, but was vacillating back and forth. He was then murdered before he could do so."

"So you think his killer was someone who paid the witness to lie in the manslaughter case?"

"Yes, which is where I am hoping Donnelly comes in."

"The theory being that Donnelly was out for your client because he was once married to his son's girlfriend?" Bowers's tone indicates he's not quite buying it.

"It's not a fully developed theory. But I'm looking for a murderer, and Donnelly's name keeps popping up. It's at the very least curious."

"That much is true." Bowers thinks for a while in silence. Finally he adds, "Look, I don't know if Donnelly is involved with your case. I'm not hearing any reason why he would be, but there certainly could be things that you haven't uncovered yet."

"An endless supply."

"Right. So let me just tell you about Paul Donnelly, and you can decide if he fits and go from there."

"Perfect."

"Donnelly is a businessman and a killer. He is without a conscience, yet in a curious way he has a code of honor. He believes that what he is doing is right, simply because he is the one doing it.

"His one weakness is what we would view as a strength. He loved his son; he worshipped that kid. So if he had any reason to believe that your client was a threat to his kid, he would step in. I don't see him as paying a witness to frame him, though. More likely he would just have him removed from the ranks of the living.

"On the other hand, if he killed your client, his son

would know that he did it and would disapprove. That might make the father think twice. By framing him, Paul Sr. could have tried to make it look like his hands were clean."

"He was there when his son was shot. Did that change him in any significant way?"

Bowers nods. "From what I have been told, he blames himself for it. Senior was the target, and Junior took the bullet. It is apparently weighing on him to the point that he's become less rational, and even more dangerous. Before he was deadly and logical, now he's deadly and partially nuts. Not a good combination."

"I'm not sure how that impacts my case."

"I'm not saying it does. What I'm saying is that if you are going to go after Paul Donnelly, be very, very careful."

have absolutely no idea if Paul Donnelly set up Chris Myers for the Bonaventura killing.

I similarly don't have any knowledge as to whether he had Charlie Burgess murdered to keep him quiet. Not only do I not know, but I do not have the slightest shred of evidence of Donnelly's involvement to present to the jury.

But what Donnelly could represent for us, if we can come up with a credible case for his involvement, is someone to point to. The jury would believe that Paul Donnelly could possibly be the murderer, simply because Paul Donnelly is, in fact, a murderer.

He is a walking, murdering hunk of reasonable doubt.

Of course, there is the fact that Bowers warned me that publicly accusing Donnelly of being a killer might not be the smartest move, from a self-preservation standpoint. I'll just have to deal with that later, if we get to that point.

For now I have to figure out how I can find evidence of a real Donnelly connection to our case. It won't be easy; it's not like I'm going to find a close associate of his that will turn on him.

The Whale is a perfect example of that. He's sitting in jail for thirty years rather than ratting out his boss. He's not doing that out of the goodness of his heart; he's doing it because he knows what would happen to him, and probably his family, if he didn't.

Eddie Dowd calls me. "I've got some good news, Andy. We hit two first-serve aces."

"What's going on?"

"Judge McVay granted both of our motions. We're going to get the discovery on the Bonaventura case, and we got a court order for the ancestry companies to run Bonaventura's DNA, looking for a match."

"That was fast. I thought we'd get the discovery, but I figured the ancestry stuff would be a struggle."

"I thought so too. But the prosecution didn't contest it."

"Big mistake." I don't know whether Daniel Morrow, the lead prosecutor, dropped the ball because of inexperience, but in my view he made the wrong call. I usually take the approach that if the prosecutor wants something, then I am by definition against it. But he chose not to follow that strategy.

The issue wasn't whether he had the ability to deny us what we want, or to talk the judge out of granting our motions, though he may have. More important, by arguing it out in court, he might have learned something about our strategy. He dropped the ball.

I tell Eddie to proceed with making the demand of the private DNA companies, looking for relatives of Bonaventura's. Eddie tells me that we will have at least part of the Bonaventura discovery by the end of today. That will give me something to do while I'm floundering around, trying to come up with a defense strategy.

Sure enough, the documents arrive at around five

o'clock. I was going to go to Charlie's tonight, but instead I'll stay home and read through them.

But I do decide to put them off until after dinner. Dinner tonight is delivery pizza; we had let Ricky decide what to get and he made an excellent choice.

But all good things come to an end, and there is a limit to how long I can nibble on the crust. As much as I don't want to spend the night going through the documents, I head to the den to do just that.

I'm almost there when the phone rings in the other room. I hope it's a telemarketer, but it isn't. I know that because Laurie answers it and says, "Hold on, Sam, he's right here." She hands me the phone.

"Hey, Sam, what's going on?"

"That's why I'm calling, Andy. There's something weird going on here."

"What do you mean?" I had momentarily forgotten about Sam's going to Metuska.

"I got to Metuska this morning. I checked into the only hotel in town; I think there is only one other person staying here besides me. At least I've only seen one."

"So? We're talking about Metuska, not Vegas. Metuska is not a Christmas vacation destination."

"I understand. It just feels deserted, that's all. I asked the guy at the desk about the eminent domain case, and he said he didn't know much about it. Which was strange, because what else has been going on in this town, you know?"

I'm already regretting that I okayed Sam going to Metuska. He's going to turn this into a Hitchcock movie.

"Maybe he just moved there. Is that all, Sam?"

"Maybe, but I asked some other questions, like if he

knew Chris Myers or Alex Swain, and I got nothing. I went out to a diner and asked the waitress about it and got nothing from her either."

"Sam—"

"I think these people are leery of talking to a stranger about this stuff."

"That's a small-town thing, Sam."

"I suppose so, but there's some kind of weird religious thing going on. They wear like a shoulder patch on everything, with some strange symbols on it."

"Sam—" He interrupts again. If all I can get out is one word, I'd better find a different one than Sam, because he's plowing right through that one.

"So I head back to the hotel, and on the way I see these guys across the street, staring at me. Big guys. They don't say anything to me, and I sure as hell don't say anything to them. I go straight up to my room and turn on my computer."

"Did we get to the weird part yet, Sam? Because—"

"It's all weird, but wait until you hear this. I go on the hotel internet, and I see that they are trying to hack into my computer."

This is interesting. Sam is never wrong about computer stuff; if he says something happened, it happened. "How do you know that, Sam?"

"Come on, Andy."

"Sorry, go on."

"So, I figured that maybe it's some hackers hoping to track some financial information if I go on any bank or credit card websites. I mean, it's not like they know who they are dealing with. But I'm overly cautious, you know? So I started looking around the room."

"For what?"

"Any sign of entry. And I found one, big-time. There were two bugs in my room."

"Bugs?"

"Listening devices, and pretty sophisticated ones. One was behind a painting on the wall, and the other was taped to the baseboard behind the bed. It's possible there might even have been more, but those two are the only ones I found."

"Whoa, Sam . . . is there any way to know if they were just put there for you, or were they always there to listen in on anyone in that room?"

"They were just put there; the glue on the backs of them is fresh."

"What did you do?"

"I left them there; I didn't want them to know that I was on to them. I went out to my car, and I found another one under my passenger seat."

"Sam, you need to get out of there."

"I already did. I disabled the device, got my stuff, and checked out. The guy at the desk asked me if there was any problem with my room. I told him that there wasn't; I just needed to get home . . . family emergency."

"Good."

"When I pulled out, the same guys were across the street, watching me."

"But you're out of there now?"

"Yes, I just left. I'm telling you, Andy, that place is weird."

told Laurie about my conversation with Sam when I got off the phone.

She agreed with me that while Sam can be prone to the dramatic, finding tracking devices in his room and car is not something normal or open to debate about how serious it might be. I told Laurie that I wanted to meet with her and the rest of the K Team in the morning to discuss next steps; they are professionals at this, and I'm just a semiretired attorney.

Laurie said she was going to make some calls, and she was on the phone for a while. At the end of them, she said we're set for a meeting here at the house at ten in the morning. I called Sam back and told him that if he can make it, I want him here as well.

At a little after nine in the morning, an old friend of Laurie's from the Paterson PD, Sergeant Wally Dickinson, shows up. I know what he's here for without his having to say anything, because he's helped us like this before.

Laurie is having him check to make sure that our own phone is not tapped, and there are no listening devices here. Her correct reasoning is that might be how the people in Metuska knew that Sam was connected to our case, if in fact they did.

It takes Dickinson the better part of an hour, but he assures us that the place is clean. The best part is that he doesn't find my stash of chocolate-covered cherries that I hide from Laurie. Laurie was a lieutenant in the Paterson PD, but she's a captain of the Calorie Police.

Corey, Marcus, and Sam arrive before ten, and I ask Sam to relate to them what he told me. Sam draws it out; he is an incorrigible and ultradramatic attention hog. This time he thinks he is doing the Metuska version of *Hamlet*.

I don't learn anything new, but I do get to see a photograph that Sam took of the four guys who were watching him. They are all large and serious looking; this was not a "welcome to Metuska" committee. They all have the patch on their shoulders that Sam mentioned, though the patches are hard to see clearly in the photograph.

Sam also shows us the listening device that was in his car, which he has deactivated. He might be prone to embellishing stories, but the device is real.

When he's done, it's my turn. "At the very least, this elevates the situation in Metuska on our list of possible explanations for Chris being framed. Having said that, it's conceivable that this is such a closed and secretive religious community that they just harbor an unhealthy distrust of visitors, especially ones asking questions."

"Those were pretty quick and drastic measures to take against a curious stranger," Corey says.

I nod. "I completely agree. But I also don't see how they could have known that Sam was working on this particular case. If they didn't know that, then we can't read too much into it."

"I agree with Corey," Laurie says. "It's an insane over-reaction to what Sam was doing. Maybe they don't know that Sam is working with us, and maybe they don't care, but I'll bet they have something important to hide."

Marcus hasn't said anything, which does not exactly qualify as breaking news.

"I'm not disagreeing, and it wouldn't matter if I was, because we gain nothing by not treating it as related to our case," I say. "If we turn out to be wrong, then no harm, no foul. So what are our next steps?"

"We need to get you to someone who has an under-standing of what is going on in Metuska," Laurie says.

"Any ideas who that might be?"

Laurie nods. "I already set it up last night. You have an appointment on Tuesday to see Captain Roger McKenny of the Pennsylvania State Police. His office is about six miles outside of Metuska."

"How did you set that up?"

"I know people who know people who know people. It's part of being a cop."

"Why Tuesday? Couldn't I do it tomorrow?"

"Tomorrow is New Year's Day, Andy."

"So tonight is New Year's Eve?"

"Yes, you party animal, you."

We spend New Year's Eve the same way every year, and this year is no exception.

Laurie, Ricky, and I had pasta and salad for dinner, then we attempted to stay up until midnight to watch the ball drop. At around ten o'clock, with us all falling asleep, Laurie set the alarm for eleven forty-five. That woke us, and we struggled to stay up another fifteen minutes to watch the stupid ball.

Then I put Ricky to bed, and he asked the obvious question. "How come we don't tape the ball dropping, and then we can watch it whenever we want?"

"You too are a party animal, Ricky."

I spent all day yesterday watching football, eating, and worrying about the case, not necessarily in that order.

We always make one New Year's resolution each. Laurie's is to eat healthier; she could stand to lose two or three ounces. Ricky's is to become a better baseball player, and mine is to retire. Mine has been the same for the last six years.

Today I'm in the car and on the way to Captain McKenny's office, equidistant between Williamsport and Metuska. It's a four-hour drive.

McKenny doesn't keep me waiting at all; he may not

be familiar with the proper police-officer/defense-attorney etiquette.

I have no idea who actually set this meeting up; I know Laurie didn't do it directly. For all I know it could have gone through twelve different cops, so I don't pretend to know the cop who finally contacted McKenny. I just thank him for seeing me on such short notice.

"No problem. Kiermeier says you're okay."

I nod. "Kiermeier's a hell of a guy." I took a chance with that; Kiermeier could have been a woman. But McKenny hasn't corrected me, so Kiermeier is probably a guy.

"So I understand you want to talk about Metuska."

"Actually, I'd rather listen than talk. I hear it's a weird place."

"That would be a pretty accurate description, unless you're one of the Fellows."

"Fellows?"

"That's what they call themselves; it's some kind of religious thing. Why are you interested?"

"Well, for one thing, an associate of mine was there the other day, not doing anything wrong, and he felt threatened."

"They're not big on outsiders; did they do anything specific to him? Does he want to lodge a complaint?" McKenny suddenly sounds eager.

"Not at this point; do you have jurisdiction there?"

"Technically, of course. I'm a state cop, and last time I looked it was part of the state. But we've only gotten one call there in the last six months."

"Why is that?"

"They have their own police department, and I think

they look at us the way they looked at your associate, like outsiders."

"Were you aware of what was going on regarding the eminent domain situation?"

He nods. "I was aware of it, but not involved. The town was acting within its legal rights, as far as I know. Some people fought it for a while, but that seemed to fizzle out. I heard a guy took off with their legal fund."

"Why does the town want the land?"

McKenny shrugs. "They say to do infrastructure stuff, roads, sewers . . ."

"And they pay good money for the land that they confiscate?"

"So I understand. I don't know why all the people didn't jump at it. I mean, who else are they going to sell to? Who would want to move there?"

"Maybe more Fellows."

"Maybe."

"Any idea where they got all this money?"

"No. Maybe religious donations? Could be they've got some rich people who believe in whatever the hell they believe in."

"Are the religious leaders in charge of the town?"

"Everything is part of the religion in that town. No one could get elected mayor or anything else unless he was a Fellow."

"So not much crime there?"

"Zero. Absolutely zero, which in itself is weird."

"Could things be happening without your knowing about it?"

He nods. "Of course. But the department doesn't go

looking for work; we've got plenty elsewhere in the state." Then, "How was your guy threatened?"

"Surveillance, and he reported four guys following him around, clearly trying to unnerve him."

"What kind of surveillance?"

"Cyber. He found listening devices in his hotel room and his car."

"If he's got evidence, I'd be more than happy to go in there. It would make my day."

"I'd rather not right now; there's a case I'm working on that could be jeopardized. But maybe you could help in another way."

"How's that?"

"I need to get in there and find out what is going on. If I have a problem with the authorities, can I call you?"

"I'll go one better. I'll call the chief of police over there and tell him a friend of mine is coming into town. He'll lay off you; otherwise he'll know I'll come in. That's the last thing they want."

"Thanks. I appreciate that."

"But I can't be sure those four guys won't bother you."

"That's not a problem; I'll be bringing a friend with me."

"One friend?"

"Technically, yes. But he has a way about him."

"Okay. Let me know when you're coming, and I'll make the call."

"Thanks. I appreciate it. Give my best to Kiermeier."

decide to go the long way back to Paterson; which means I will take a leisurely drive through what I'm sure is lovely downtown Metuska.

It's only about fifteen minutes away, so I figure that while I am there, I can briefly get what Sam and Chris both referred to as the lay of the land.

There is one sign off the small highway for Metuska, with an arrow pointing east for three miles. There is no mention of any food or fuel to be had there, no hint of a McDonald's or Taco Bell, no Hampton Inn or Best Western inviting travelers to spend the night.

I pass a small WELCOME TO METUSKA sign and enter what must be the main area of the town. The best way to describe it is nondescript; the houses are clearly inexpensive, but reasonably well maintained and not in disrepair. The cars are certainly not luxury models, but neither are they wrecks mounted on cement blocks in driveways.

I pass the Hotel Metuska, the cleverly named place where Sam stayed. It's a fairly narrow three-story building, and I don't see much if any activity when I look through the glass door and windows. Farther on ahead is the police department, with one squad car parked out front.

The church is by far the most impressive building in

town, with a sign simply saying THE HOUSE OF THE FEL-
LOWSHIP. I see few people, and most of the ones I do see
are wearing the patch on their shoulders that Sam described. But it's fifteen degrees outside and starting to
snow a little, so I wouldn't think that many people would
be out and about.

Sam's four-person "welcome squad" is nowhere to be seen
either. Of course, I haven't stopped and asked any questions;
I'm just driving through.

I don't see any children, not even in the small park with
swing sets and other stuff that kids would ordinarily flock
to. The basketball court is empty as well. It's four thirty
in the afternoon, so I suppose everyone might still be in
school, but I doubt it. Moments later I drive by the School
of the Fellowship, but it does not seem to be in session;
no one is around, and only three cars and no buses are in
the parking lot.

I notice a lot of equipment and what looks like pending construction in some places. In a large dirt field is a
sign saying FUTURE HOME OF THE METUSKA TIGERS, but
there's no indication that any progress has been made in
building that home.

Another large area seems to be under construction, but it
is behind a solid fence, so I can't see what might be in there.
I see men with patches that almost seem to be guarding
this area, but the fence should do an adequate job of that,
since there aren't exactly invading armies trying to pierce
the perimeter.

On the way out of town I pass Metuska Mills, a medium-
size factory. It's gray and somber looking, in keeping with

the rest of the town. At least thirty cars are parked there, so the factory must be operating.

Then I'm out of town, so I make a U-turn and go back through. I'm no longer trying to learn anything; I'm just heading toward the highway that will take me back to Paterson. Metuska has proven to be anything but exceptional, and I would question whether Sam was just being overly dramatic, if not for the listening devices.

I call Laurie and describe my conversation with Lieutenant McKenny, and his promise to call ahead and clear the way for me.

"So you think it's worth going back?"

"I think so. If Sam is off base, then it's just a day wasted. But if I shake up things by asking questions, maybe I'll provoke the same response."

"Or worse," she says. "One of us has to go with you. I would suggest Marcus."

"So the choice is eight hours round trip alone in a car with Marcus, or not bringing Marcus and risking death? It's a tough call."

"Then I'll make it for you. Marcus goes."

"You think you can run my life?"

"I do."

"Okay, Marcus goes."

"Now that that's settled, I have some interesting news for you," she says. "You got a phone call today."

"From a telemarketer, I hope?"

"Not exactly. It was from Paul Donnelly Sr. looking to talk to you."

"He called personally?"

"No, but it's possible he was going to get on the phone if you were around. He's calling back tonight at eight o'clock."

"Any idea what he wanted?"

"I asked, but the guy wouldn't say. But you'll find out at eight o'clock."

"I hate talking on the phone. And talking on the phone to organized crime bosses is the absolute worst."

"You can mention that to him when he calls."

The phone rings at exactly eight o'clock.

Paul Donnelly may be a killer, a drug dealer, a thief, and may run illegal gambling and prostitution operations, but he's certainly punctual. That is an admirable trait.

I am nervous as I pick up the phone. I don't even get out my charming "Hello" opener before the voice on the other end says, "Carpenter?"

"That's me."

"Paul Donnelly wants to see you."

"No problem. Tell him to google my name and click on 'images.' But let him know that the camera makes me look fat. I don't know why that is."

I have over time learned that when dealing with people like this, the worst thing you can do is appear intimidated. That is a problem for me, since I am thoroughly intimidated, but I fake it by being a wiseass. For me, being a wiseass is not exactly a creative stretch.

Laurie is in the room listening to my end, which makes me want to sound even more confident. It's embarrassing to have her hear me when my voice shakes.

"What the hell are you talking about?" The voice is a husky, deep one. I would be willing to place a large bet that this guy has no neck.

"Which part didn't you understand?"

"I told you that Paul Donnelly wants to see you."

"Well, it turns out that I don't want to see him."

"You want me to tell him that?" The guy sounds more incredulous than threatening now; apparently Paul Donnelly gets to see whoever he wants.

"I don't care what you tell him. Put him on the phone and I'll tell him myself."

"Carpenter, you are making a hell of a mistake. Nobody says no to Paul Donnelly."

"I just did; I thought you heard me. But let me give you a clear message. If he wants to meet with me, that means he has something to tell me or ask me, right?"

"I don't know what he wants, asshole," the guy says, moving from incredulous to pissed off.

"Well, I'm betting he doesn't want to play tennis or exchange recipes. So let's assume he wants to talk. If that's the case, tell him to call me and we can talk all he wants. In fact, I have some questions for him."

Click.

The guy was apparently tired of talking to me and hung up.

I hang up the phone and turn to Laurie. "I think I made a new friend."

"I'm sure you did. Why did you change the plan?"

Laurie and I had decided that if Donnelly wanted to meet, I'd agree to it, but only in a place and situation that ensured my safety.

"I'm not sure; it just felt right in the moment. The guy pissed me off."

"I'm sure you haven't heard the last from Mr. Donnelly."

"That will give me something to look forward to."

I call Sam, who starts with "I got it."

Laurie had come up with the idea of telling Sam to bug our phone and tape what we thought would be a conversation with Donnelly. Sam is letting me know that he accomplished the task.

"It's probably just the preliminary round. Can you keep recording more calls as they come in?"

"Sure. You think they'll call back?"

"I hope so. It's better than if Donnelly decides to shoot me and get it over with."

"There is always that possibility."

"Thanks, Sam."

My cell phone on the night table says 1:58. I am looking at it because the ringing of the phone just woke me up.

My body clock is not perfect, but I am pretty sure it's not 1:58 in the afternoon.

This simply cannot be good news.

Did I mention I hate telephones?

I look at the caller ID and it says PRIVATE CALLER. I hope it's someone suggesting I renew my car warranty or buy aluminum siding for my house. But I'm afraid I know who it is.

"Hello?"

"It's Paul Donnelly." My fear is confirmed.

"It's also two o'clock in the morning."

"Tell me something I give a shit about. My man says you refused to meet with me."

"I thought we'd chat on the phone first . . . you know, get to know each other. I don't like to rush into relationships; slow but steady is my motto."

"Russo says you're an asshole."

He's seems to be referring to Joseph Russo, Jr., his counterpart in North Jersey, who I have had my share of clashes with. I had no idea guys like this were part of a network. "You talked to Joseph Russo about me?"

"Yeah."

"What is this? Six degrees of Don Corleone?"

He ignores the question. "Listen carefully. Do not bother Jessica. You got that?"

"Jessica? You mean Jessica Myers?"

"That's right. I do not want to hear that you bothered that girl again; it would make me very upset. You do not want me upset with you."

"She told you I bothered her?"

"She told me you were asking questions. I don't want you asking her questions; I don't want you talking to her."

"How about if I ask you the questions instead?"

"How about I put a bullet in your head?"

There's not really a good answer for that, so I ignore it. "What do you know about Charlie Burgess?"

After a pause, he finally says, "I don't know who you're talking about."

"Okay, what about Chris Myers, Jessica's first husband?"

"He's in jail."

"You put him there, by killing Bonaventura and Burgess."

"Russo said you were an asshole; he didn't mention that you are also full of shit. But don't accuse me of anything, you understand? Stay out of my business, and stay away from Jessica."

"What about the Whale and the RX and More deal? Why did you need Chris Myers out of the way?"

"I don't give a shit about Chris Myers, or you, or

Burgess, or Bonaventura, whoever they are. . . . I am telling you to leave Jessica alone, leave my business alone, or you will be meeting with me, whether you want to or not. And it will be a really short meeting."

Click.

"What was that?" Laurie asks, now wide-awake.

"Wrong number."

"Andy . . . I know it was Donnelly. What did he want?"

"He wants me to leave Chris's ex-wife alone. She told him I was asking questions."

"That's all?"

"That's all."

"Okay. Let's talk some more in the morning. This is sleep time."

"I won't be able to sleep now," I say.

"I will."

"Won't the sound of my heart pounding keep you up?"

She shakes her head. "No, I can sleep through anything."

I didn't get back to sleep until around three o'clock and woke up again at seven. It's because of Paul Donnelly that I will be tired all day.

I think I'm going to let him slide this time; it's possible he was busy ordering killings and stuff and lost track of the time.

Today I am back at Everson, Manning & Winkler to talk to Victor Everson. He made the offer, probably insincere, to entertain specific questions about things that Chris was working on. That's what I'm here to do.

This time he keeps me waiting in the reception area for twenty minutes; I think the Andy Carpenter glow may have dimmed somewhat in his eyes. That happens a lot.

The Christmas tree is still up in the reception area, and the blinking lights are getting on my nerves. I wonder if the date they take it down is in some corporate handbook, or if it just comes down whenever Everson, Winkler, and Manning get tired of it. Maybe the three of them vote on it.

While I'm waiting, Harold Caruso, Chris's old friend, colleague, and drinking buddy, walks in. He comes over and says hello before heading back to his office.

I finally get into Everson's office, and after about thirty

seconds of meaningless chitchat and how are you's, he asks how Chris is doing.

"Hanging in. Quite well, considering how difficult it must be to be imprisoned for something he didn't do."

"I'm sure it would be." Everson's "would be" means that he strongly doubts Chris's innocence.

"So I have some questions about business Chris was working on. There shouldn't be any confidentiality issues."

"Hopefully not. Fire away."

"Let's start with the Harkin Pharmaceuticals case. My understanding is that the RX and More suit was dropped because the Feds busted them."

"That's correct."

"How far did it go before that happened?"

"I believe we were early in the discovery phase."

"Chris was supervising that phase?"

"I would be surprised if he was. But he was part of the team."

"A crucial part?"

"Everybody plays a role, but it's unlikely Chris would have been in any way indispensable. His performance had been slipping by then." Everson shakes his head. "Very sad."

"Can you think of any reason that RX and More, or Harkin for that matter, would have benefited greatly from Chris being removed from the team?"

Everson thinks for a moment. "No. None."

"Are you familiar with the case Chris was working on in Metuska, Pennsylvania?"

"Barely. I believe it involved eminent domain?"

"Yes. The townspeople hired you to fight the city of

Metuska and prevent them from taking their land and homes."

"Right," he says with no conviction, as if he doesn't remember the case all that well.

"So you're not familiar with the particulars of the case?"

"I'm afraid not."

"Can Harold Caruso join us? Maybe he could save time and fill in some of the blanks."

Everson looks surprised; he obviously wasn't aware that I knew Caruso took over some of Chris's work. "I don't believe he's in."

"Unless he has a twin that also works here, he's in. I saw him get off the elevator."

"Is that right," Everson says, more as a statement than a question. He picks up the phone and tells someone to ask Caruso to come in. Within sixty seconds, we're a threesome.

"Harold, this is Andy Carpenter. He's representing Chris Myers in that criminal case."

Caruso just nods; he doesn't seem anxious to let Everson know we are old buddies. "So how can I help?"

"Mr. Carpenter has some questions about Chris's work in . . ." Everson can't seem to remember the town.

Being ever helpful, I throw in, "Metuska."

"Yes, Metuska. Mr. Carpenter?"

"How did they come to hire your firm?" I ask.

"I really don't know," Caruso says. "But we've done a lot of work in that area of the law, so if they asked around for a firm with experience and an excellent track record, I'm certain we would have come highly recommended. But I wasn't involved at the inception of the case, so I don't think I ever knew how they came to us."

"Did you and Chris work on it at the same time?"

Caruso nods. "Yes, although Chris was in the lead position. I just backed him up when he . . . when he wasn't paying total attention."

Caruso apparently doesn't want to sandbag his friend in front of their boss, even though Chris's previous drinking is certainly no secret, and Everson is no longer Chris's boss.

"Did you know Alex Swain?"

Caruso's face takes on something between a smile and a grimace. "Oh, yes, I certainly knew Alex Swain."

"Do you know why he left town?"

"Because he is a son of a bitch. He called me; this was when Chris had already left. He said that we shouldn't expect to be paid any more, because he had sold his house and left town."

"He had already left?"

Caruso nods. "Yes. The caller ID showed he was at a Ramada in Indiana. I asked him what was going on, and he laughed and said I should consider this a 'courtesy call,' and that I wouldn't be hearing from him again."

"What did you do?"

"There was nothing to be done with him. I went to Metuska to talk to the people who were part of the lawsuit to see what could be done. They were stunned that he bailed on them; they considered him a friend. It was sad to see."

"So they couldn't pay to keep your firm on the case?"

"No, but to be perfectly honest, they may have saved money in the long run. It was a tough case. In situations like this the entity invoking eminent domain has the presumption of legality, and they usually prevail. There was nothing in this case to make Metuska an exception. But we were fighting the fight."

"Do you know if the townspeople reported Swain to the police? He embezzled their money."

Caruso nods. "That's what I told them to do, and they said they would, but their hearts didn't seem to be in it. I think they had had enough and were ready to move on. It was tough to see."

Everson frowns slightly and starts shuffling papers on his desk. That's always a sure sign that someone wants a meeting to end; he's subtly announcing that he has these papers that are just begging for imminent attention.

"Do you remember the names of any people you spoke to when you were there?" I ask.

"No, afraid not. They were a committee, so there were maybe six or seven people. Most of them were women. It wasn't a long meeting; like I said, they seemed ready to give up."

"Do you see any reason why anyone would have benefited from Chris being removed from the case?"

Caruso laughs. "Just me. If Chris hadn't left, he would have been the one meeting with those people. But, no, that case had mostly run its course when Swain bailed on them."

"Anything else you need to know, Mr. Carpenter?" Everson asks.

"No, that should do it," I lie, since I have an endless supply of things I still need to know.

Unfortunately, I'm not going to find out any of them here.

Based on everything I have heard, there is nothing going on in Metuska, Pennsylvania, that should interest me.

Harold Caruso would have been in a position to know if something untoward had happened, and he says that there was nothing. Not even Chris, albeit with an impaired memory, can think of any reason why the source of his problems should reside in Metuska.

Certainly I didn't see anything particularly unusual when I drove through, but I wouldn't have expected a sign across Main Street saying WELCOME TO METUSKA, THE TOWN THAT FRAMED CHRIS MYERS. Still, it seemed like Normal Town USA, with some shoulder patches thrown in.

On the other hand, someone was suspicious enough to go to the trouble of bugging Sam's room and car.

It could have had nothing to do with Sam's being on our team. Maybe it's just a highly secretive group of religious wackos who see danger to their way of life behind every corner.

Maybe they are distrustful of every stranger who comes into town. It's legitimate for them to wonder why a visitor, without any ties to anyone in the community, would show up in the first place. I can't imagine there is anything to do there. Metuska is not Disneyland; they may wear shoulder patches, but they don't wear ear hats.

But someone was trying to hack into Sam's computer.

Unfortunately, when it comes to areas we have to attack, we are not in a target-rich environment. Paul Donnelly is a more likely candidate, but he has served notice that I might wind up being the target. All we have is his peripheral involvement with Chris, certainly nothing jury-worthy.

Still, four guys were watching Sam, and it made him feel threatened.

It doesn't take a mathematician to add it up. Bugging plus hacking plus threatening, minus few other suspects, means we have to look further into Metuska.

It also means a road trip with Marcus Clark.

Four hours will seem like four years.

Each way.

We're going to go tomorrow, so I call Captain McKenny and ask him to place the call to the chief of police in Metuska. "Don't mention that we're coming tomorrow. Just say that my friend and I may be coming to town, and that he should watch out for us. Make it casual."

"Okay, but then he might not react quickly. You could run into the same difficulties that your friend did."

"We'll be able to handle it."

"If not, call me. They do not want us in their town, so I'd like an excuse to go in."

"Thanks, Captain."

My next call is to Sam, asking him how we can protect ourselves from being surveilled while we're there.

"I'll get you a device you can use to sweep the room and your car. Marcus knows how to use it."

"Okay, good."

"You and Marcus going to share a room?"

"I'm thinking not."

Laurie calls Marcus and tells him the game plan. We are going to leave at 6:00 A.M. That way maybe we can get enough accomplished in the one day to get the hell out of Metuska by early evening.

I take the dogs for their evening walk and break the news to Tara that Laurie will be taking them on their morning walk. Tara seems okay with it, as does Hunter. I think Sebastian is just disappointed to hear that there will even be a morning walk.

I'm not going to Metuska with a fully thought out plan for what I am going to do there. Certainly I'll ask questions, and I will probably look up a schoolteacher that Chris said he found helpful. She may have left town already; her house may even have been taken from her.

I'll basically play it by ear. Sam apparently elicited a reaction simply by asking around, so I will do the same. Certainly Marcus's presence will help me attract attention.

Marcus picks me up at 6:00 A.M. sharp. I get in. "Good morning, Marcus."

He says something in response; I can't tell if it's a grunt or a word. I only recently found out that Marcus speaks normally; he never showed that side to me before.

But that hasn't impacted our conversations much; he still hardly speaks, at least to me.

I'm not surprised to hear classical music on the radio when I get in the car. I learned about Marcus's musical tastes on a similar drive a while back. It's not my thing, so I will be able to avoid any desire to start tapping the dashboard to the beat.

We stop at a Dunkin' Donuts along the way. I get a coffee and a blueberry muffin. Marcus gets two large coffees, two buttered bagels, an egg sandwich, and three bran muffins.

If I didn't know Marcus, I would think he was planning to feed a platoon of soldiers just up the road, but he eats it all himself. He does this while driving, but instead of criticizing him for doing something dangerous, I clench my teeth and hope for the best. Unfortunately, it's difficult to eat a blueberry muffin through tightly clenched teeth.

I use the time to go through some of the information that Sam got from hacking into the law firm's files, paying particular attention to the Metuska case.

I'm interested to see that Chris had conversations with someone named Peter Fornes at the Pennsylvania Bureau of Land Management. Chris's notes say that Fornes was sympathetic to the case and was going to look into it. There is no mention of any resolution, or if Fornes actually conducted an investigation. By the time that would have happened, Chris had already been arrested for having killed Bonaventura.

Just before we get to Metuska, I call Sam and ask him to get me a phone number and address for Fornes. If Chris met with Fornes or just spoke to him, Fornes might possibly have a better recollection of the circumstances than Chris does.

The plan is for us to have lunch at a diner I had seen in town as I drove through the first time. Sam said he asked questions there and suspiciously got nothing in response, so I'll do the same.

When we arrive in town, I tell Marcus to head for the hotel. They have a small parking lot in back, so we pull in there and go around the building to the front of the hotel. I want to get a room now, so as to give them ample time to plant any bugs before we get back, should they be so inclined.

We no sooner get out of the car than it starts to snow. Many towns look pretty when snow is falling; Metuska is not one of them. Instead of looking gray and depressing, it looks white and depressing.

When the two of us enter the hotel lobby, it brings the total number of people in the room to three, including the guy behind the desk. "Can I help you?" he asks in apparent surprise that anyone has walked in.

"Sure can. Two rooms, please. Suites if you have them."

He only has one suite, so I graciously give it to Marcus. I'm hoping we don't spend the night here anyway, but that is still to be determined. I brought a small suitcase, mainly to carry the sweeping device that Sam gave me. Marcus has a duffel bag.

We bring the stuff up to our rooms, and Marcus immediately comes to my room, according to plan. He is going to use the device to determine whether any bugs are already in the room; if there are not, but we find some later, we will know that we are the specific targets.

Before he uses the device, Marcus checks for any hidden cameras. He doesn't find any, so he uses the device to check for bugs. There are none; the room is clean.

Marcus then goes to do the same to his room, then comes back. "Clean."

"Okay. Metuska, here we come."

We walk the length of the downtown area, which is only three blocks.

It's no more revealing than my drive through was the other day; Metuska feels like a town where people have low expectations, and the town makes no effort to exceed them.

There is a bar, but a glance in through the window shows it to be either empty or closed. Not too surprising for noon on a weekday. There's a small library and a couple of restaurants, in addition to the diner. No fast-food places, not a golden arch to be found.

We pass the City Hall, a small, unimposing building with five cars in the parking lot. The church is certainly the most impressive structure in town, but only because Metuska sets a low bar for impressive buildings.

We double back and enter the diner. Of the twelve tables, seven are occupied. Not everyone is wearing the shoulder patch, but all the men are.

As one of two waitresses is passing by, I say, "Two for lunch," and she points to an empty table near the window.

Marcus and I sit down at the table; the menus are already there. In New Jersey, diners have menus that could barely fit into the Library of Congress. Metuska handles it differently; there aren't many choices, and the ones here are the basics. Meat loaf is what passes for exotic cuisine.

The waitress comes over to take our order; her name tag says CLARISSE.

I say, "Nice town, Clarisse."

"Yeah. What are you having?"

"I'll have the burger and fries, no cheese, and my friend will have two orders of the meat loaf."

"Two orders?"

I nod. "To start."

"What brings you to town?" she asks.

"House hunting."

She does a slight double take. "In Metuska?"

It seems to me that men at the adjacent tables are trying to overhear our conversation, so I speak a little louder to help them out. "Yes, seems like a nice, quaint community. But the one thing that worries me is that I heard the town started taking people's land from them a few years ago. I wouldn't want that to happen to us."

"I don't know anything about that."

"You weren't here then?"

"I don't know anything about that." Her voice is low and she looks like she wants to be doing anything rather than talking to us.

"Any suggestions on who we could talk to that would know something about it?"

"No." She walks away.

I don't know if she's the same waitress that Sam spoke to, but the result is certainly the same. Clarisse does not look like she just got off the bus in Metuska this morning, and people at other tables are referring to her by name.

If I had to bet, I'd put money on her having been here from well before the eminent domain stuff went down; she just doesn't want to talk about it or is afraid to.

I notice that the guys who were listening in get up and leave well before we do, which I am pleased about. It will give them time to spread the word.

Marcus and I walk outside and I check a map of the town that I found online. It's still snowing; at least an inch is already on the ground.

Sam had learned the address of Denise Holman, who I believe is the teacher Chris said he had met with here. He said that when he was briefly in town, Alex Swain was unavailable or away, so Ms. Holman showed him around.

He thought she was a fourth-grade teacher, so I suspect she won't be home, but it can't hurt to stop by and see. Walking through town is also an end in itself, in that I want us to be seen.

We reach Holman's house, which is not far from where a lot of construction is taking place. It's less than a block from the fenced-in construction area. It seems like the work is mostly on this side of town, though it may extend to the other side when it's finished.

We ring the bell and I'm surprised when a woman comes to the door. She's probably in her forties, pleasant looking and probably someone that central casting would send down when the call came for a fourth-grade-teacher type.

"Denise Holman?"

"Yes."

"My name is Andy Carpenter, and this is my associate Marcus Clark. I'm an attorney, and we'd like to talk to you about a case we are working on."

"You're not going to get anywhere."

"I'm sorry; I didn't understand that."

"Aren't you representing the town?"

"Actually, nothing could be further from the truth. I suspect you'll find out that we're on your side."

"If you are, you'll be the first in a long time. Come on in."

So we do. I notice that before she closes the door, she looks up and down the street to see if anyone is watching.

This seems promising.

Once we're seated in her den, I tell her that we are representing Chris Myers in a case that may have its origins in Metuska.

The name Chris Myers doesn't register for her until I tell her that he was a New York lawyer representing the townspeople.

"Oh, yes. I remember him now. He came here when Alex was away, and I showed him around. What happened to him?" Then, without waiting for an answer, "I suppose he lost interest when Alex took off with the money."

"That's sort of what I'm trying to determine. Why hasn't the town taken your land?"

Her laugh is short. "Because so far I've stopped them, but that won't last long."

"You've been fighting it?"

"We all were for a while, until Alex left. I never thought he would do that, turn on his friends in that way. One of the great disappointments of my life."

"Why do you think he did it?"

"Money. There is plenty to be had if one wants to go along."

"But you don't?"

She shakes her head. "I don't."

"Why?"

She thinks about it for a few moments. "Two reasons, I guess. One is that I care about the children, although so many have left town with their families that there aren't many remaining. My class size has gone from twenty-eight to eleven."

"And the other reason you haven't left?"

"Because they want me to."

"Who are 'they'?"

"The Fellows, as they call themselves."

"Not the town government?"

She smiles. "They are one and the same."

"Who is the leader of the Fellows?"

"The official title is high pastor. His name is Samuel."

"Last name?"

"He never uses it, just goes by Samuel. But he had to list it in a court filing, so I know his last name is Fulton. On the rare occasions I've had to talk directly to him, I refer to him as Fulton. I think and hope it annoys him."

This is my kind of lady. "How long have the Fellows run the town?"

"They showed up about three and a half years ago. You wouldn't know it, but this was once a normal, albeit economically depressed, community. Then they sold the factory to the Fellows, and nothing has been the same."

"But people have been paid decent money for their homes?"

"Better than decent, though homes in Metuska are not exactly high-ticket items." Then, looking at Marcus, "Mr. Clark is the strong, silent type?"

Marcus smiles. "I am." It's a veritable conversational explosion from Marcus. He must also like her; Marcus is partial to fighters, and this woman is definitely one.

"Why are they so anxious to spend all that money to get people out?"

"They claim it's to do improvements in the town, but I think it's to 'purify' it. They only want people who practice their religion to live here."

"Are they doing the improvements?"

She shrugs. "So they say; there's a lot of activity, but if you see any new roads or buildings, let me know."

"So how have you been trying to hold on to your house?"

"Well, I don't have the money to pursue it with a lawyer, not since Alex took off. So I am trying to do it myself. The Bureau of Land Management has been no help, so I filed a brief with the court." She smiles. "I googled how to do it."

I take a card out of my pocket and hand it to her. "I'd be honored to represent you."

She looks at it. "Did you miss the part about my not having any money?"

"That's okay, I have more than I need. Look me up online and call me if you want me to be your lawyer."

"Thank you, I will." She looks hopeful but a little wary; she's obviously been burned in this process before.

My goal in making the offer was twofold. For one thing, this woman needs help, and I would like to take a shot at providing it. For another, having a client in the fight gives me standing to deal with people I might want to deal with, both in government and out.

"By the way, do you know how Alex Swain came to pick Everson, Manning and Winkler?" I ask.

"That's the law firm in New York?"

"Yes."

"I think Alex said that they heard about our situation and approached us, but I'm not too clear on that."

We get up to leave.

"How long are you going to be in town?"

"Not very long; we'll be leaving today or tomorrow."

"Please be careful. Strangers are not at all welcome around here."

"So I've heard. We'll be fine."

She smiles. "I'm going to google you now."

"Don't click on images. The camera adds ten pounds."

Another smile. "I've become all too aware of that. It also adds ten years."

Marcus says, "Call him; you will not be sorry."

I can't seem to get Marcus to shut up.

We leave and I'm about to call Laurie when I see that Marcus is staring intently at something. I look across the street and slightly down the block.

Marcus had seen them before I did. It's four guys, like the four Sam described, watching us.

I think Sam was right.

There is something wrong in Metuska.

We start walking in the opposite direction from the foursome, and while I imagine they are following us, I don't look back to check.

I take out my cell phone to call Laurie; at least out here on my phone I can be sure no one is listening in.

I briefly tell her what has gone on, then ask her to call Sam. "Tell him to find out anything he can about the Fellows or the Fellowship, and their leader, a guy by the name of Samuel Fulton."

"Is there anything specific you want to know?"

"I'm most interested in where they are getting all their money. They've been buying houses and land, and doing construction. None of that comes cheap."

"Anything else?"

"Yes, see if Sam can get Fulton's phone number to monitor his calls. It might be interesting to know who a high pastor talks to."

"Okay. Have you seen the men that Sam felt threatened by?"

"They're watching us even as we speak."

"Stay close to Marcus," she says, once again showing less than total respect for my physical prowess.

I hang up, and we keep walking. We're not far from the construction activity, though it is blocked off by fencing.

Interestingly, the fence is solid wood, not chain link, or we would be able to see inside. That could be by chance, or they might not want anyone to see what's happening in there. I've got an idea for how to get around that if it becomes necessary, but for the time being it will have to wait.

Even though they are trying to remain unobtrusive and in the background, clearly men are walking near the fence as guards. They are all wearing those patches, and without a doubt keeping an eye on us as we approach the fence.

I knock on the fence as I would on a door, and a big guy with a patch comes over to us. "Can I help you?"

"Sure can. My friend and I were wondering, is this fence oak, or pine?"

"This is private property." Not the most responsive answer to the question.

"I say it's oak; he says it's pine. It sounds like oak when you tap on it."

"Move along."

I knock on it again, and I turn to Marcus. "You hear that? Definitely oak. Pine has a more hollow sound." Then I turn to the guy with the patch. "If you find out, let us know, okay? We're at the hotel. Have a good day."

Marcus and I start to walk away, and I say, "I know oak when I hear it."

We start taking a different route back to the hotel. As we turn, I see that the original four guys who were following us are still there.

"Let's talk to them," Marcus says. Apparently he doesn't

like anyone to think he can be intimidated. I'm learning more about Marcus by the minute.

"Not yet. But I've got a feeling we'll get our chance."

We walk toward the church, and as we approach, the door opens. A few people are leaving, so we decide to take advantage of the open door and go in.

A large guy is standing near the entrance, wearing some kind of robe, with the obligatory patch on the shoulder. If this were a bar instead of a church, he'd be the bouncer. "Who goes there?"

"'Who goes there?'" I repeat. "Did you learn that in the movies? And isn't it supposed to be 'Halt, who goes there?'"

"This is private property."

Apparently this town is filled with private property. "So your church isn't a welcoming one? All we want is to come out of the cold and perhaps receive some warm porridge and a kind word before we go on our way."

He doesn't respond to that, so I try another approach. "Can we talk to Samuel? Maybe he'll be friendlier."

"What is your name?"

"Andy Carpenter. I'm the high pastor of Paterson, New Jersey. You can tell him we'll be quick."

He goes off for a few minutes. When he comes back, to my surprise he says, "Follow me. The high pastor will see you."

As we start to follow him, I turn to Marcus. "I hope you like porridge."

We're led to a small office, not in any way what one would expect of the high pastor. Sitting there is a guy in a robe, patch on his shoulder. He looks to be in his early forties, tall and thin.

"Welcome. My name is Samuel."

I notice that Bouncer is staying in the open doorway.

"Thanks for seeing us. This is Marcus Clark."

"How can I be of service?" Samuel talks in a peaceful, serene, calming tone of voice . . . which immediately gets on my nerves.

"Why is your church taking everyone's land?"

He shakes his head, as if sad to hear this. "I had hoped you were better informed. The actions you are referring to are undertaken by the city, not our church."

"I'm told you run the city."

"You are mistaken, Mr. Carpenter."

"Okay, then why is the city taking everyone's land?"

"To make municipal improvements, I believe. Perhaps you should be at City Hall asking these questions, rather than here."

"It's necessary to run everyone out of town?"

"I sense a hostility; I hope I did nothing to provoke it."

"You live in hope. Do you know Chris Myers?"

"I don't believe so."

"He is an attorney who tried to stop you and failed."

"Why are you telling me this?"

"Because I am an attorney who will try to stop you and won't fail."

"Good day, Mr. Carpenter, Mr. Clark. Brother Miller will show you out."

The bouncer, now known as Brother Miller, turns and starts walking. We don't follow for a couple of reasons. For one, I don't want Samuel to think we take orders from him. For another, I want to see how far Brother Miller will walk before he realizes he's all alone.

Once he's out of sight, I smile and say to Samuel, "Brother Miller might be lost. Anyway, just so you know, we'll go wherever we want, whenever we want to."

"You are no longer welcome here."

"Heartbreaking. By the way, if you're the high pastor, does that mean there are pastors lower than you?"

He doesn't answer, so I say to Marcus, "Let's go," and we walk out, passing the confused Brother Miller on the way.

We've certainly done all we can do to be annoying, so we head back to our hotel to see if the rooms have been bugged.

The four shoulder-patched goons follow us from a distance; I wonder if this is their regular job. What do they do when there are no strangers in town? Practice by watching each other?

Marcus uses the sweeping device in my room, and in about thirty seconds he locates two bugs. We don't bother removing them because we have no intention of staying here tonight. Instead we'll go to the diner, see if we can ask any more questions, then leave town. We'll probably drive all the way home tonight, but if not, we'll stop along the way.

We could stop at a forced-labor gulag and it would seem more hospitable than Metuska.

The lunch and dinner menus are exactly the same, as are the waitresses and most of the patrons. It's like we've stepped onto a movie set during the filming of the scene, and this is take two.

Clarisse the waitress comes over. "You find a house?"

"Oh, yes . . . a lovely two-bedroom Cape Cod. Needs a little work, but I think we can be very happy here. It even has a playroom for little Marcus. Does the church sponsor bingo games? Samuel didn't say."

She does a small double take at the mention of Samuel's name, but just asks us what we want to eat. I get a hamburger and small salad; Marcus gets two more meat loaf plates with mashed potatoes and three pieces of pie for dessert. His diet is going well.

The waitress brings the check. "Good luck with the house."

"Thanks. Now we just have to wait on the mortgage."

Softly, so that I can barely hear her, she says, "Watch yourself."

I don't know if Marcus heard her, but it doesn't matter because Marcus always watches himself.

By the time we leave, it's been dark out for a while. We walk back to the hotel and I don't see our four followers anywhere. That means they are probably not watching us because before this they've made no effort to conceal themselves. I think the whole point was to intimidate us, and that requires them to be out in the open.

"We're going to be checking out now," I say to the desk clerk.

"Something wrong with the room?"

"No. We just realized you don't have a casino. My friend loves baccarat; he's quite good at it." Then, "You can email me the receipt."

"Okay."

We get our bags. I'm tempted to take one of the bugs with us, but I don't know what that will accomplish. It won't tell us anything about who planted it, and it will only alert our adversaries that we are on to them. It might in the future benefit us for them to think they are successfully surveilling us.

We walk around the building to our car, parked in back in the parking lot. It's quite dark back here; the only light is from some of the rooms inside the hotel. But there's enough light for us to see the four goons waiting by our car.

One of them is actually sitting on the front hood in the snow that has accumulated on it. The rest are leaning against it casually. These guys are not worried.

I am.

Even though I'm with Marcus, these situations unnerve me. I always have to remind myself that the worst thing I can do is show that nervousness. The best way not to show it is to be a sarcastic wiseass. That I can do with no problem whatsoever.

"What are you guys doing here? Is there an asshole convention in the hotel?"

This seems to get their attention; they stand a little straighter, and the guy on the hood slides off. My instinct tells me that he is the leader.

"We don't like your kind around here."

"That is heartbreaking to hear; we tried so hard to fit in. Now move away from the car before you get hurt. You guys are ugly enough as it is without having your faces smashed."

He smirks; I hate people who smirk. "Is that what you're going to do? You and your quiet, dumb friend here?"

Marcus doesn't react to that. He is at his most dangerous when he doesn't react, and also when he does react.

Marcus is at his most dangerous pretty much 24–7. I'm counting on that now.

"Okay," I say to the guy who slid off the hood. "You're obviously not bright enough to understand what's going on. I don't know you guys; is there a non-imbecile in the group?"

No one answers, so I say, "That's what I figured. Now get the hell away from the car."

Hood Guy begins moving toward us threateningly. He starts to say something, I think it begins with "Time" or maybe "I'm," but it's hard to be sure. That's because Marcus has elbowed him in the throat, and all he can do is make gurgling noises. Then Marcus slams Hood Guy's head back into the top of the hood, and he stops making noises altogether.

The other three seem stunned at the suddenness and ferocity; I know I am and I expected it. One of them seems to back off slightly, so Marcus heads for the other two.

In the dark it's hard to tell exactly what happens, but after some screaming and groaning, they are both on the ground, lying in the snow, as silent as Hood Guy.

Marcus turns to the fourth guy, who is holding up his hands in surrender. If he had a white flag, he'd be waving it furiously.

"We're cool, okay? I don't even know these guys."

"Who sent you?" I ask.

Suddenly, rather than answer, he turns and runs away, toward the street. He apparently has no qualms about leaving his three friends behind.

He's a coward. . . . I can respect that.

Laurie is waiting for me in bed when I get home. Okay, she's sound asleep, but I choose to think that she's resting so she'll be refreshed to greet me.

But she does become wide-awake when she asks me how it went, and I tell her we were attacked by four goons. I describe how it went down, slightly embellishing my involvement in the fight.

In my version, I rained punches down on the bad guys, but there is absolutely zero chance that she believes me. I can tell that because after I finish, she asks, "So Marcus handled all four of them?"

"He did, but I was there in case he ran into problems. We decided to keep me in reserve."

"Good decision. Good night."

The first thing I do in the morning, after taking the dogs for their walk, is to head down to the jail to talk to Chris.

"I just spent a lovely day in Metuska."

"You did? Is that place a key to our case?"

"Might be. You need to think back to that time. Think of it as picking your own brain."

"Okay."

"In your files, you mention that you spoke to a guy named Fornes at the Bureau of Land Management."

Chris thinks for a while. "I did. I think I went to see him. His office is in Philadelphia."

"Why did you go to him?"

"I wanted to get the state involved. The town was pissing me off; they had no interest in talking or negotiating. And I felt bad for the people who were being displaced. So I was trying to go over the head of the people in the town."

"What did Fornes say when you talked to him?"

"He was interested; at least that's how I remember it. I don't know if he fully believed me; I mean, I was a lawyer representing a client. But he didn't like how it sounded and said he would look into it."

"Why didn't he like how it sounded?"

"Because the town hadn't presented detailed plans for what they were going to do with the land. Eminent domain is only permitted in cases where there is a public good arising from it, meaning infrastructure improvement, that kind of thing. The town had not demonstrated that they had a plan like that."

That is consistent with what I found in the files. "Did you ever meet Samuel Fulton, the guy they call the high pastor?"

"No. Pretty much everyone in the town gave me the cold shoulder; they were not prepared to engage on any level."

"Do you have any idea where they are getting their money? They are buying up homes and land at an above-market price and doing construction. A lot of money is going out, rather than coming in."

Chris shrugs. "I know they are running that factory. I think they're making religious stuff; those things can sell pretty well, no? Or maybe they have some wealthy people as part of the religion."

I spend another fifteen minutes with Chris going over some trial preparation. Usually I have to instruct clients on how to behave; in this case Chris is going to be hearing some pretty bad things said about him, and I don't want him to react in any way.

I also don't want him making eye contact with jury members, but nor should he always look away from them. Chris already understands most of this since he was a lawyer with trial experience, and he has been on trial already himself. But criminal trials are about leaving nothing to chance, so I want to make sure he is prepared for everything.

When I leave the jail, I check my cell phone and find a message from Sam. I call him back.

"I found Fornes."

"Is he still with the Bureau of Land Management?"

"No. And I can't find any record of him working anywhere else either. I have his home address and number if you want it."

"I do."

Sam gives it to me; Fornes lives in Haddonfield, New Jersey, not too far from where his office had been in Philadelphia.

Sam says, "I'm still checking on where the Fellows get their money. It's complicated, but I'll spare you the details for now."

"Okay. Laurie asked you to check on Fulton's phone calls, right?"

"Yes, that's also a little complicated. There is no record of Fulton having a home address; he gets his mail at the church. I'm betting he lives there as well."

"Is there a phone?"

"No landline, but there are a few cell phones that are in there most of the day, and one that is still there at night."

Sam can tell by accessing phone company records where any cell phone is at all times through the GPS that all phones carry.

"I think for the time being we should assume that the one there all night is Fulton's. But just to be sure, call Denise Holman in Metuska, tell her you work with me, and ask her if she knows where Fulton lives."

"Will do."

"In the meantime, track who Fulton calls and has called over the last few months. We left there about five o'clock yesterday afternoon, so I'd be particularly interested if he made any calls around then."

"I'm on it, Chief. Anything else?"

"Yes, one more thing. I didn't see anyone else in the hotel when Marcus and I were there."

"Yeah, I told you I only saw one other person."

"Can you get a list of everyone who has stayed there in the last six months? They must be computerized; they're going to email me a copy of the bill." I keep piling stuff on Sam, but he handles all of it.

"Shouldn't be a problem." Then, "I was right about Metuska, wasn't I?"

"You were definitely right."

"Did you run into those four guys?"

"We did. And they ran into Marcus."

"I am very glad to hear that."

Next I call the number Sam gave me for Peter Fornes. He answers and I tell him who I am, and who I'm representing. I ask if I could meet with him, and he agrees with no persuasion necessary. In fact, he seems pretty eager, and I tell him I can be down there in a couple of hours.

I'm getting a little tired of these long road trips, but at least I don't have to listen to classical music this time.

W ith the radio mine and mine alone, I get to listen to the talking heads on ESPN endlessly debate where Aaron Rodgers is going to play next year.

They also are discussing Tom Brady's retirement and unretirement, which I must say I find a bit insulting. I've retired and unretired way more than Brady, and they never mention me.

Since Rodgers and Brady do not play for the Giants, I am not that interested in their employment status. So I just treat it as background noise and focus on what I have learned about Metuska, and the likelihood that it's relevant to our case.

I think the secret to all that has happened to Chris may well be buried in Metuska. Certainly something sinister is going on there. Not just because of the way strangers are treated, but to follow the money is to watch it all move in one direction.

The town of Metuska, backed by the Fellows, has paid out a small fortune and received no money in return, at least not that I can see. This makes no sense; the idea that they are buying all those houses to make municipal improvements has to be nonsense.

The surveillance and the fact that the goons attacked us

and intimidated Sam only adds to the feeling that something bad is going down in that town, and that they don't want anyone digging further into it. We have absolutely no evidence that any part of that involves Chris, but we'll keep digging.

The other possibility remains Paul Donnelly. While I think it is far less likely that he brought these problems crashing down on Chris, he is still our best bet to use on the jury.

A jury would have little trouble believing that Donnelly is capable of bad acts. A strange religion in a Pennsylvania town is less credible on its face as the perpetrator, and it would be more of an uphill struggle to get the jury to believe it.

Having said that, a bigger concern is that whichever alternative killers I present to the jury, I have no evidence. I currently know nothing that Judge McVay would rule admissible; I just can't back it up. Which is a problem, because the trial is staring us in the face.

By the time I reach Fornes's house, I'm so depressed about the state of the case that I'm back to listening to ESPN, which has moved on to who might be the first pick in the NFL draft, which is three months away.

This season isn't even over yet, and they're talking about next year. It would be like Chris's trial not even starting yet, but me looking on to my next client.

God forbid.

Fornes lives in a development of homes built in a way to make none of the residents living there jealous, since they are all exactly the same. If the houses didn't have numbers on them, the homeowners would wander the streets aimlessly, wondering which house was theirs.

Fortunately, they do have numbers, and my GPS gets me to the right house without any problems. Fornes hasn't spent much time shoveling, icing, and salting, so it's a little difficult navigating his walkway and steps, but I manage slowly.

The door opens before I get there, and he is waiting for me, smiling. "Sorry about that. My back pain and laziness precludes a lot of shoveling. And I don't get many visitors."

"No problem."

We head into the house.

I follow him into the kitchen. He opens the refrigerator. "I've got coffee, cold pizza, salad dressing, and I think I have some salt somewhere in here. Anything interest you?"

"What kind of salad dressing?"

"Thousand Island, although it might be expired down to four or five hundred island."

"Then let's go with the coffee."

He puts a pod in his Keurig coffee maker, and, presto, I have a cupful.

"So when did you leave the Bureau of Land Management?"

"Oh, you didn't check me out?"

"Not sure what you mean."

"I was caught up in a sexual harassment scandal. A woman came to see me, allegedly about an issue she was having with a company encroaching on her farm. I told her I would check into it, she left, and that afternoon she said I tried to force myself on her."

I already have questions, but I'm going to wait and let him finish his story. A man accused of sexual harassment who denies those charges is not exactly unprecedented.

"She was lying through her teeth. But nobody, and I mean nobody in management, took my side. These are people I worked with for twenty years; they were just too damn scared to support me. The whole thing was a setup. And I proved it, at least to myself."

"How?"

"Because after I left I checked out her story. No farm, no company, no encroachment . . . just a lot of horseshit. And I don't mean on the farm. She was sent in by someone to set me up."

If Fornes is telling the truth, then moving him out of the way on a bogus charge certainly parallels what happened to Chris. "Any idea who or why?"

"None. But just try to get another job after something like this happens. I've got a lawsuit pending, but I doubt it will get anywhere." He shakes his head in obvious disgust, something I am sure he has done many times. Then, "So you wanted to talk about Metuska?"

"I do. My client, Chris Myers, said he talked to you about it. I'm curious though . . . how long after you talked with Chris did this sexual harassment thing come up?"

He smiles knowingly. "I looked up the case when you called; I had taken digital copies of my files with me; I thought it might help in a lawsuit."

"Smart."

"I had forgotten all about Metuska. The woman came

to my office five weeks after I met your client. You think the two things could be related?"

"I think it's very possible. What did you think of the situation and what did you do about it?"

"I thought it was bullshit; the town was taking all this property without legitimate plans for what they would do with it. They were acting like damn dictators; that doesn't fly with me."

"Did you take any actions?"

"I notified the mayor that I was starting an investigation, and that he should preserve all relevant materials and documents. It's standard procedure."

"What happened next?"

"I heard back from them that they would follow my directive, and that they were confident I would find that everything was in order."

"And then?"

"And then that woman came to my office."

"Do you know who was assigned to the case after you left?"

"I heard from some friends there that they didn't hire anyone to replace me. My boss picked up some of it, and the rest was assigned internally. It was probably my boss, but I can't be sure."

"What's his name?"

"Arthur Hagan . . . the prick. He totally bailed on me."

All the people who were in any way involved in fighting the town of Metuska seem to have been moved out of the way.

Chris went to jail for the death of Bonaventura, Alex Swain was bought off for what must have been a lot of money, Peter Fornes was fired from his job on a sexual harassment claim, and Charlie Burgess was shot in his own house.

I can't be positive that Fornes is telling the truth about being innocent of the harassment charge, but if he is, it fits in neatly with what happened to Chris and Swain. Fornes told me that he worked at that agency for twenty years, and suddenly he gets accused for the first time soon after commencing an investigation into Metuska.

I don't buy it.

With a trial looming, I always try to do some normal things, knowing that soon there won't be time for them. So after my morning walk, I take Laurie and Ricky for a Saturday breakfast at the Suburban Diner on Route 17. We spend most of the meal laughing; the atmosphere is like it was at the diner in Metuska, except totally different.

After breakfast we pick up Tara and Hunter and head down to the Tara Foundation to play with the dogs. I ask

Sebastian if he wants to go, holding up the leash and encouraging him. He looks at the leash; I think he's trying to decide if it's edible. But then he lays his head back down; he's going to sleep this one out.

Going to the Foundation is a real treat for Ricky; he's become a total dog nut like his parents. Tara and Hunter gravitate to the puppies; they are growing, and that seems to fascinate them. Killian, the mother, looks on proudly at her offspring.

As we head home, Eddie Dowd calls me with some bad news. The ancestry services did not turn up any family matches for Joey Bonaventura, if that's even his real name.

I'm not too disappointed because at the time we submitted it, I thought that the goal might have been to kill Bonaventura, not to get Chris out of the way. I thought maybe Chris was just an easy foil.

I no longer consider that a viable possibility. Metuska has convinced me otherwise; they were trying to remove Chris from the eminent domain case. I now think that Bonaventura, whoever he is, was the one in the wrong place at the wrong time; he apparently died simply to get Chris arrested and convicted.

When we get home, Sam is waiting for us. This can mean a couple of different things. One is that he's hungry; Sam lives alone and doesn't cook for himself much. Two is that he has something to report.

Numbers one and two are not inconsistent, and that turns out to be the case here. He has something to report, but would be happy to chomp down on some sandwiches while reporting. Laurie asks if he wants roast beef or chicken, and he says, "Yes."

I negotiate a deal with Sam. He can eat the chicken sandwich, then must give us his report before he can eat the roast beef. I deliberately structured it that way so that he will give us the report quickly and succinctly, since roast beef is his favorite.

It takes slightly more than a nanosecond for the chicken sandwich to disappear, as I knew it would. Laurie, understanding my strategy, positions the roast beef sandwich where he can see it, but it's out of arm's reach.

"What have you got, Sam?"

"Okay. The Church of the Fellows takes in very little money; if they seek contributions from their members, they are small. But they have set up a shell corporation, based in South Africa and called Enterprise Holdings Ltd., which takes in plenty of money."

"South Africa?"

"Yes. And then that corporation makes its donations to the church, which they use for their operations. The church also pays a great deal of money to the town of Metuska, both in taxes and donations. I assume that is how the town has funded the eminent domain purchases; I don't see much other source of income for Metuska."

"Where does Enterprise Holdings get its money?"

"Mostly from the Cayman Islands. But the transfers are anonymous and secure; the source is impossible to determine. But these people are taking a great deal of care to conceal their financial transactions, and they are sophisticated at it."

Sam continues, though I think he is drooling as he stares at the sandwich, "They have an office in Metuska, but according to Google Maps, it's a storefront with no name outside, and I certainly didn't notice it."

"I didn't either, and we just about walked the whole town."

"The corporation also has a private jet, which they keep at an airport about fourteen miles from Metuska. I assume it's for Samuel Fulton's use, but I don't know that."

"What about his phone?"

"I called Denise Holman, who said that she's sure that Fulton lives in the church. She also told me to tell you that she googled you, and she happily accepts your offer. She'll be calling you."

"What offer is that?" Laurie asks.

"To represent her against the town. I'm taking on clients, right and left. Like a lawyer. Go on, Sam."

"I also checked out the religion itself, or at least I tried to. It doesn't seem to be anywhere else than Metuska, and I can't find any history before it arrived there. It seems to have just sprung up. Also, if they are trying to recruit followers, it's pretty subtle. I haven't seen any evidence of it."

"It's like a cult, with Fulton as the leader," Laurie says.

"Right. So I concentrated on Fulton, and because he lives in the church building, I focused on the phone that stays there at night. Fulton does not make a lot of calls, and he didn't make any after you left. I'll keep monitoring it, but so far I found two calls that I thought were interesting."

"What's that?"

"He made them to a guy in New York by the name of Anders Regis."

"Weird name; who is he?"

"He's a leading broker in rare and valuable gems, mostly diamonds."

"What does a guy like that do?"

"He doesn't have gems of his own; if you want to find a stone of a particular type or value, he finds it for you. We're not talking about your run-of-the-mill engagement ring; we're talking about big-time stuff."

"So the high pastor of Metuska has a private plane and a taste for expensive gems," Laurie says.

I nod. "Hallelujah."

Denise Holman calls to hire me to be her attorney, just as Sam told me she would. "Why didn't you tell me you were famous?"

"If I was really famous, I wouldn't have to tell you. You would have heard of me. Besides, I'm a humble sort."

"I have very little money to pay you."

I tell her I'll charge her my normal fee, minus a 100 percent discount.

"That doesn't seem right."

"I'm sorry, I can't do better than one hundred percent off. I have shareholders to answer to."

She laughs. "Do you think you can help me?"

"I'll certainly try. Overnight me all the documents you have so far, then write up absolutely everything you know about what the town has done in that area. If you have friends who have sold, or who haven't, tell me whatever you know about their experiences."

"Okay, I will."

"And tell me whatever you can about any construction you know the town has done so far."

"Hard to know. It's all behind that tall fencing."

What she's just said reminds me of something I thought

of while I was in the town, but stupidly forgot to follow through on.

I tell Denise that I will review the documents and get back to her about next steps. As soon as I hang up, I tell Laurie my idea. I think we should find someone to use a drone to fly over the construction site and photograph what is there.

"Great idea," Laurie says. "Call Corey; he told me the other day that he went out with a friend who flies them. He says the video they take is amazing."

I call Corey and he confirms what Laurie said, and he's sure that his friend would be glad to help out. He says that he'll come right over to go over the plans.

I hang up. "Corey's coming over."

Laurie nods. "I'd better make more sandwiches. Come on into the kitchen; we need to talk about something."

I haven't conducted a survey, but I doubt that anyone, anywhere, has enjoyed a talk that someone told them they "need to have." It's more than counterintuitive; it's by definition impossible. Good conversations are ones you want, not need, to have. Just like you *want* to have fattening desserts, but you *need* to go on a diet.

"Sit down," Laurie says, another ominous warning sign. When people want you in a particular position to hear what they have to say, it is never good. If you're on the phone with someone who says, "Are you sitting down?", you'd better not only sit down, but brace yourself against a table.

"Let's assume for the moment that there's something criminal going on in Metuska," she says. "And I know we can't prove it, but let's further assume that Metuska is the source of Chris's problems."

"Okay, both are probably true."

"Yes, they are. And while we're in assuming mode, let's add to the assumptions that the town has managed to move out, by various means, anyone who has gotten in their way. They got Chris arrested, they bought off Swain, they got Fornes fired, and they killed Burgess and probably Bonaventura."

I know where she's going, so I just sit back and wait for her to get there.

"Who's in their way now?" She doesn't wait for an answer. "You are."

"Laurie, those four goons were buffoons. Even I could have handled them, if I were a completely different person."

She smiles, but she doesn't think it's funny; she is a woman on a mission. "Leaving aside the question of what might happen if you tangled with a single buffoon without Marcus present, you're not seeing the actual picture."

"I'm not?"

"No. Remember what the bookmaker, Dinardo, told you? That the guys who recruited Burgess to lie were probably connected and were dangerous. Dinardo has been around; he knows dangerous when he sees it. And Burgess's friends in the alley told us that those guys were scary as hell."

"I do recall that, yes."

"Andy, if the source of all this is Metuska, then the four guys Marcus took apart were the junior varsity. The first team killed Bonaventura and Burgess, and they were professionals."

"So . . . ," I prompt, so as to get to the resolution.

"So I'm calling Marcus."

Laurie and I have been through this many times, far more than should be necessary for a lawyer. The next time I win the argument will be the first.

"I forbid you to call Marcus."

This draws a loud laugh from Laurie. "You forbid me?" Clearly she considers the concept hilarious.

I shrug. "I thought I'd take a shot." I'm not sure when Laurie and I had our marital power struggle, but I'm certain that I lost it.

"You did, and it missed. But there's more. These people are not only dangerous; they're sophisticated. The way they got rid of Chris and Fornes showed it. You need to be alert to them coming at you in a way you don't expect. Asymmetric warfare."

She's right, so I don't argue the point, which is just as well. My record at winning arguments with Laurie is somewhat worse than the Knicks' record at winning basketball games.

Preventing me from suffering further humiliation, Corey shows up. "What's to eat?"

While Laurie makes him sandwiches, I draw a rough map of Metuska, basically to show him where the construction site is. He has with him overhead photos of the town from Google Maps, which makes my map drawing basically unnecessary.

"It's important that you not be seen," I say. "I don't care if they see the drone, which they obviously will. They won't have time to conceal anything. Once we have the photos, that's all I care about."

He points to an area outside town, not too far from the construction area. "We should be able to set up here. The drone has plenty of range to cover that distance. We'll get in and out fast, in case they try to shoot it down."

"Shoot it down? This is Metuska, Pennsylvania, not North Korea."

Corey gives me a dirty look, but Laurie defuses the situation by putting a sandwich in front of him. Laurie's sandwiches are the ultimate peacemaker.

Just before Corey chomps into it, he says, "We'll fly it tomorrow. It will be fun."

"More fun than I'll have," I say. "I'll be in court."

I hate jury selection. Everybody claims to be an expert, but no one has any idea what they are talking about.

I try to approach it logically, but basically I go with my gut. Unfortunately, my gut has absolutely no idea what it's talking about.

The worst part is that after the selections are over, I have no feeling at all for how I did. That answer doesn't come until the end of the trial, when the verdict is read. By then the ship has sailed.

I can compare it to a roulette wheel. For one thing, no one who plays roulette has a clue what they are doing; it's all luck. But imagine you were playing roulette, and someone else was picking the numbers for you. And further imagine that they didn't tell you what numbers they picked for you until after the wheel was spun, the ball landed, and it was over.

So you had no idea what to root for while the wheel was spinning; you weren't going to find out the result until it was done. You think that would be fun? If you do, you'd love jury selection.

Chris has experience at this as a litigator, but it's a completely different situation from what happens in a murder trial. He doesn't volunteer opinions on individual potential jurors; he says he trusts Eddie and me to make the right decision.

If he only knew that we are completely winging it.

We get the jury seated in just one day, an extraordinarily fast process by normal standards. There are seven women, six Caucasians, four African Americans, and two Hispanics.

It's a diverse, open-minded group, or at least one that claims to be open-minded. I'm not sure I've ever met a completely open-minded person in my life, yet we are alleged to have seated twelve of them? I don't think so.

Today is Thursday, and the jury won't be called back until Monday. Tomorrow morning will be reserved for the judge and the lawyers to address the key question of the trial, whether testimony regarding Chris's manslaughter conviction will be admissible.

There is no telling how long that will take, certainly not all day, but Judge McVay is still planning to start the trial fresh on Monday.

Eddie Dowd has written, and we have filed, what is called an in limine motion. It seeks to prevent any mention of the manslaughter arrest, trial, and conviction. If the motion is granted, Joey Bonaventura's name will never be mentioned in this trial, and the fact that Chris served fourteen months for his death will not reach the ears of the twelve people we have just selected.

I think we are probably going to lose, but we need to try.

When I get home, Laurie tells me that Corey and friend have accomplished their drone mission and are on the way back to Paterson. Corey should get here with the video after dinner.

I go on my evening walk with our dogs through East-side Park; it's the time when I can think most clearly. I focus on what my argument will be for the in limine motion tomorrow.

Whether the information about Bonaventura will be allowed in is crucial. It is the only thing that connects Burgess to Chris, and Burgess's testimony against Chris, and Burgess's belated refusal to recant it, represents the prosecution's entire theory of motive.

The park is dark tonight; it's cloudy so the moon is nowhere to be seen. I have no idea if Laurie has already put Marcus on to protect me, but she probably has. The fact that I don't see him anywhere has nothing to do with the darkness; Marcus is only seen when he wants to be.

I must say that I don't feel like I'm in any danger, Marcus or not. Metuska feels light-years away from Paterson, and even though I know that the Bonaventura and Burgess murders were committed here, it somehow doesn't feel like the Fellows have that kind of reach.

Sebastian is getting slower and slower; one of these days he is just going to refuse to move and I will have to call Triple A and have him towed back to the house. But we finally make it back, and Corey is waiting for me in the den, along with Laurie.

Ricky is also there, but Corey says that it's fine. He's looked at the video, and there's nothing Ricky shouldn't see. Obviously the drone didn't pick up a mass grave of murder victims.

Somehow, and this is way beyond my technical expertise, Corey is able to show us the video on our television.

The video is amazingly clear, and what it shows is thoroughly puzzling. They have dug a huge rectangle in the ground; according to Corey it's probably a hundred feet by seventy five feet, and at least forty feet deep.

In the middle of it is another hole, maybe twenty by twenty-five feet, which goes farther down. It's impossible to tell how deep that hole is from the footage we see.

"That looks like an elevator," Ricky says, earning his salary.

Corey nods. "Could be."

Off to the side, outside the rectangle, is another hole, no more than ten feet square. Again, we cannot tell how deep it is, or its purpose.

Surrounding everything are at least ten trucks, which Corey somehow identifies as cement trucks. We can only assume that the massive hole that's been dug will be filled in with cement.

I don't know what all this is for, but they could bury a lot of Jimmy Hoffas in a hole this big. And whatever it is, it's important enough to be well guarded. As Marcus and I saw, men are patrolling all around it.

One thing is for sure: we are not looking at the "municipal improvements" that the town promised.

I don't know how this can be useful to us in the trial, but it can certainly be helpful to my other client, Denise Holman.

've read your briefs, so let's get started," Judge McVay says. "Mr. Carpenter? It's your motion."

As I stand, I realize I am in a weird position, maybe the first time I've ever been faced with this situation.

We're in a gray area. Chris's past manslaughter conviction would ordinarily have no place in this trial; it is more prejudicial than probative. The problem for us, and the reason the judge may rule against us, is that it goes to motive.

Another way to look at it is if Chris had been convicted of manslaughter in a case that had nothing to do with Burgess, one in which Burgess did not testify. Then clearly the conviction would not be admissible here. But because Burgess's testimony provided a motive for Chris to hold an intense grudge against him, it might well come in.

One factor in our favor is that judges tend to give the benefit of the doubt to the defense because an appeals court might overturn the conviction and order a retrial if it feels an error was made. It is impossible to overstate how much judges hate when that happens.

But the reason this position is so unusual for me is that I might not want to win. I don't mean initially; I wouldn't have filed the motion if I didn't at this moment think we would be better off prevailing. Burgess testifying against Chris at the earlier trial provides a perfect motive, and it would be devastating for the jury to hear it.

But—and it's a big but—this could change down the road. If we can get enough evidence to introduce the Fellows of Metuska or Paul Donnelly as alternate possible murderers, then the landscape changes entirely. Because the frame-up that we would be alleging spans both crimes. We would have to show that Burgess was paid to lie for the bad guys to have had a reason to kill him now.

But as was famously said, you go to war with the army you have. Right now our army, our weapons, do not include enough evidence for Metuska or Donnelly to be admissible, so we have to proceed as if we will not have it. If we come up with something later on, I'll deal with it.

"Your Honor, with all due respect, our motion should not be controversial. There is ample case law on the subject; as you know, we referenced numerous cases in our brief. The previous conviction of Mr. Myers should not be a matter to be presented to this jury. It is clearly more prejudicial than probative."

I'm not on terribly firm ground; most of the cases we cited did not deal with motive, which is a major factor here. A few of them did, so we have a shot, but I am not confident.

The judge turns to the prosecution table. "Mr. Morrow?"

"Your Honor, this is not a typical situation to decide whether a prior bad act is admissible. In this case, the previous conviction provided a clear reason for Mr. Myers to hold a grudge against Mr. Burgess; he expressed it openly to a number of people.

"Not letting the jury know about the history between these two men would have the effect of blindfolding the jury. It is obviously relevant and obviously probative, and we have also provided case references, as I know you are aware."

My turn next. "Obviously our position is clear, Your Honor. However, if you feel otherwise and are inclined to admit the testimony, then I would ask that it be sanitized."

"Explain that, Mr. Carpenter," she says.

"I mean that if a witness is to say that Mr. Burgess testified against Mr. Myers in a prior proceeding, then the nature of that proceeding should not be referred to. It should not be said to be involuntary manslaughter. That would send the prejudicial nature of this into the stratosphere."

Obviously Morrow is opposed to this, and we bat it around for a while, but I think that we are going to get our ass kicked. The truth is that we should lose; even though we believe Chris is innocent, common sense would dictate that the jury should know about his prior relationship with Burgess. Otherwise, why did he even enter Burgess's house?

Judge McVay says that she will retire to her chambers to consider the matter and will be back soon to announce her decision. When she says she will "retire," I have to admit that I'm envious.

She comes back and her decision is short and not so sweet. "Evidence of the defendant's previous conviction will be admitted in trial, as will his previous relationship and interactions with the victim. While I understand the always-present tension in matters of these kinds, the determining factor in my decision was the impact on potential motive.

"The testimony will be full and complete, not, as Mr. Carpenter described it, 'sanitized.' See you Monday."

Chalk one up for the bad guys.

When I get out of court, I find three messages from Sam, each subsequent message more urgent than the one before it. The last one is "Andy, you need to call me as soon as you can."

So I do, and Sam doesn't beat around the bush. "Andy, I've been monitoring Fulton's calls, and about three hours ago, he made a beauty."

"Who did he call?"

"Paul Donnelly."

Kaboom.

With all the thinking I have done about this case, and I've been so focused that I've barely watched the NFL playoffs, I never considered that Paul Donnelly and Metuska could be connected.

I saw them as separate entities, both possible factors in Chris's situation, but not part of one large conspiracy. It didn't seem possible, so much so that I never once gave it a thought.

Obviously I should have.

Samuel Fulton, who is just about the czar of Metuska, called Paul Donnelly. That doesn't just happen. Many millions of people can spend their whole lives without ever calling Paul Donnelly.

According to Sam, the call lasted for eight minutes. This was not a "Sorry, wrong number" situation.

Sam had taped Donnelly's call to me, at my instructions, and had kept the phone number. He amazingly recalled it and recognized it when Fulton called that number. Sam is worth his weight in pancakes.

In a case that has been filled with doubt and uncertainty every step of the way, this development removes a great deal of it. There is no question now that something about Chris's work caused his problems; that work is the connective tissue between Donnelly and Metuska, as Chris was assigned to cases involving both of them.

There is no longer any doubt that Metuska is deeply involved, and the same can be said for Donnelly. When Donnelly called to threaten me; he had told me to stay away from Jessica Myers, but he also told me to stay out of his business. He wasn't calling because he had a soft spot for her; that was just a diversion. He was really warning me to stop interfering in his affairs.

The destruction of Chris Myers, and Donnelly's interest in Metuska, for reasons I have still to discover, were the affairs I was being told to stay out of.

I want to get the K Team together to discuss this and go over our next steps, but I can't right now. I'm on my way to Philadelphia to meet with Arthur Hagan, Peter Fornes's boss when Fornes was at the Pennsylvania Bureau of Land Management.

Hagan was surprisingly willing to meet with me when I had called. I guess land management in the state is slow these days. But it's another five-hour round trip; I wish I got frequent driver miles for these excursions.

The bureau occupies one floor in a midtown office building. It's typically government issue—drab, cheaply furnished, and like pretty much every other government building I've ever been in.

Hagan's office is one of ten surrounding a bullpen full of cubicles, of which maybe half have people currently in them. I've arrived at about 4:00 P.M., so I don't know if some have gone home. But Hagan is in, which is all I care about.

"Thanks for seeing me on such short notice."

He smiles. "Well, I've heard of you, so call me curious as to what you could want."

The Carpenter fame is interstate. Today Pennsylvania, tomorrow the world. "What I want is to talk about Metuska."

"What is a Metuska?"

"It's a town consisting of land for you to manage."

He smiles. "I was only kidding. What about Metuska?"

"I was talking with Peter Fornes a few days ago."

"Uh-oh." Hagan adds a frown in case I didn't get the message. "Peter bears something of a grudge against me and this agency, and the world for that matter. He believes he was wronged, or at least claims so."

"I'm not representing him."

"Who are you representing?"

"Denise Holman, a resident of Metuska. She does not want to give up her property for a bogus land grab."

"That's a serious accusation."

"I'm aware. But well supported by facts. Mr. Fornes was handling the case when he left. I'm trying to learn what happened to it after that."

"As I recall, and I would have to check the files, we determined that the town was well within its rights. They were making municipal improvements, which is within their purview. We only intervene in cases like this when laws are being violated."

"Did you handle it yourself when Fornes departed?"

"I believe I did. It did not take intensive investigating."

"It's been almost three years; would you like to see the progress they've made on their municipal improvements?"

He seems surprised. "If it means traveling to Metuska, that would have to wait a while. I—"

"It doesn't. I can give you the quick thirty-second tour." I take out my phone and press the buttons that Corey told me to press. Then I hold the phone in front of Hagan so he can watch the video.

When it's finished, he asks, "What is that?"

"Good question. I know what it isn't. It's not roads, or schools, or sewers, or pipes. Maybe you can do a more intensive investigation. In the meantime I'm going to court to try and encourage you."

His voice turns considerably colder; the thrill he felt at meeting the famous Andy Carpenter seems to have abated somewhat. "We will handle this according to procedure."

"Like last time?"

I'm not sure what to make of Hagan. Possibly he's an overworked, barely motivated bureaucrat who just didn't consider Metuska important.

It's also possible that Fornes was sandbagged so Hagan could take over the investigation. And then perhaps Hagan was persuaded to take less of an interest in the case. It doesn't make much sense to get rid of someone and then wonder whether his replacement will continue causing problems.

But whatever the reason, Hagan paid little attention to the situation and did not follow up at all. The reason for that will take its place on the list of things I still have to learn.

Corey, Marcus, and Sam are at the house with Laurie when I get back. Corey and Sam are in the kitchen eating, which does not exactly qualify as a news event, while Marcus is in Ricky's room playing video games with him.

Ricky calls him Uncle Marcus, and Marcus is clearly crazy about Ricky. I am the only person in the family, dogs included, who is scared to death of Marcus.

I'm sure Laurie has told Marcus she wants me guarded 24–7. Since I think even people from the planet Krypton have to sleep, I suspect that Marcus has recruited Willie to take on some of the guarding responsibility. Willie would never admit it to me, so I don't bother asking him.

I've asked everyone to be here so we can plan our next steps. I'm going to have to lean on the group more with the trial starting. Obviously I'll be in court pretty much all day every day, and the outside investigations cannot miss a beat, or, to paraphrase Sonny Corleone, I'll be approaching the jury with only my briefcase in my hand.

I ask Sam to bring me up-to-date on his online research; I've become dependent on him.

"I've got the list of guests at the Hotel Metuska. As we both noticed, they have almost no guests. In fact, in the last three months just eleven people have stayed there, and that includes you, me, and Marcus. I don't know how they stay in business."

"They must be subsidized by the Fellows. You have a list of the guests?"

"I do; I have a copy for you, but to me only one of them is interesting."

"Who is that?"

"A guy name Clifford Heyer; he stayed there for almost ten days a few weeks ago."

"Why is he interesting?"

"A couple of reasons. By the way, he was the other guest who was there when I was. I googled photos of him and I recognized him. But he never was charged or paid a bill at the hotel; he was obviously comped."

"What's the other reason?" Laurie asks.

"He's a prominent scientist and a professor at MIT. His field is nuclear physics."

"What the hell is a nuclear physicist doing spending

ten days in Metuska?" I ask of no one in particular. "Metuska does not seem like a hotbed of scientific studies."

"Could be anything," Laurie says. "He could be Fulton's cousin for all we know. Or he could have gone to Metuska for Christmas vacation knowing he wouldn't have to fight any crowds."

I nod. "Maybe Metuska hosts spring break for eggheads."

"I'll go up to Boston to see what I can find out about him," Corey says.

"Great idea. But don't approach him; I don't want him knowing we are interested in him until we have a better idea what's going on. We can't confront him too early. Just find out whatever you can."

"Got it. I'll head up there tomorrow . . . hopefully back with a report by Monday."

"Okay, now for the big question. What is the connection between Metuska and Samuel Fulton and Paul Donnelly?"

"Well, not to state the obvious, but Chris and his law firm represented a connection," Laurie says.

"Which makes the firm interesting to us, and probably Everson in particular. He's the one who assigned Chris to both cases. But we also know that Fulton and Donnelly have been in touch with each other. I doubt that Donnelly has found religion."

"Donnelly could be a source of funding for him," Corey says. "The money for what they've done in Metuska has to have come from somewhere."

Laurie nods. "And Donnelly also is providing the muscle. The four dopes in Metuska didn't kill Bonaventura and Burgess and set Chris up. That was done professionally, and Donnelly would have the people to pull it off."

"So that's what Fulton gets from Donnelly," I say. "That's logical. But what does Donnelly get from Fulton?"

"Has to be money," Corey says. "What else could he want?"

"But we just said he's probably supplying the money. He's the supplier and the receiver?" Laurie asks.

"It could be an investment now for a payoff later. But we need to figure this out," I say. "Immediately."

Everyone who has a speaking role in a trial—lawyers, judges, witnesses—is different in the courtroom from how they are in real life.

I've met lawyers outside, in social or business settings, who I consider ineffectual and unimpressive, but when they get up to speak to a jury, they dominate a room with their charm and gravitas. And the opposite has been true: people who are the center of attention in every other room they enter lose that luster in court.

When I was in his office, Daniel Morrow was just another guy. But today, when he stands up to give his opening statement, he's lighting up the room. I hate lawyers not named Andy Carpenter who light up the room.

Morrow has a style like mine in that he likes to walk around the courtroom when he speaks, rather than stand behind a lectern. But he always keeps his eyes on the jury and talks without notes. A lectern is set up in the center, but during this trial it's going to be strictly an observer; no one is going to use it.

"Ladies and gentleman, first of all, thank you for your service. I mean that sincerely—you have a huge responsibility, and I hope what you get out of it is a feeling of accomplishment and pride." He smiles. "Because you're not going to get rich from it; I think you know that by now.

"I know none of you expected to be starting the new year sitting on a murder trial jury, but here you are. And all of us appreciate it.

"There are certain things we have a right to expect, all of us, and at the top of that list is safety in our homes. We do certain things to ensure that, just in case. We lock our doors, some of us install alarms, some even keep firearms for protection.

"But the bottom line is that when we are home, we want to be safe and secure . . . we deserve that. It is part of the life, liberty, and pursuit of happiness that is in our Declaration of Independence. It is, in fact, an unalienable right.

"Charles Burgess wanted to be safe in his own home, and I suspect that he assumed he was. It was turning towards evening; he had switched on the television, had his dinner, and was most likely settling in for the night.

"Moments later he was dead, lying in a pool of his own blood, the victim of a bullet in the head. A man . . . that man, Christopher Myers, had come in through an open window and taken his life.

"This was not a random entry, nor was it even a burglary. Mr. Myers had harbored a grudge against Mr. Burgess for three years. He testified against Mr. Myers in an involuntary manslaughter trial those three years ago. He was an eyewitness to it, and there is no doubt that Mr. Burgess's testimony went a long way towards securing a conviction. And there is certainly no doubt that Mr. Myers knew that.

"In the intervening time he made no secret of his dislike and resentment for Mr. Burgess. Clearly those feelings came to a boil and he exacted his revenge.

"Mr. Myers wasn't coming over to play bridge. As a general rule, if you are home and someone who hates you enters unannounced through a window, you need to be wary of what that visitor is planning.

"Mr. Burgess was surprised, and he was unprepared, and he paid the ultimate price for it. He lost his life, he lost his liberty, and he lost his pursuit of happiness. Mr. Myers took that all away from him, and we will show you evidence to prove it."

My watching Morrow on center stage is depressing enough, but watching the jury intently hanging on his every word is even worse.

"So thank you again, and please bear with me and stay awake if I present dry evidence that leans towards the boring side. I wouldn't be offering it to you if I didn't think it was necessary for you to do your job.

"It is too late to give Charles Burgess the safety he deserved in his home, but it is not too late to give him belated justice.

"Thank you."

Morrow sits down. I don't know if he's pleased with his performance, but he should be. The guy is good. Chris is trying to maintain an impassive expression, as I coached him to do, but I can see that he's shaken by what he has just heard.

My turn.

"Ladies and gentleman, I also want to thank you for your service, and in case you're keeping score, that is the last thing that Mr. Morrow and I will agree on during this trial.

"That's what trials are about: two sides presenting competing visions, so that you get to decide who is right. My side has a slight advantage, granted not by the Declaration of Independence but by the Constitution. That advantage rests in the fact that for you to align with Mr. Morrow's version of events, you must be positive that he is right. You must be sure beyond a reasonable doubt. Otherwise you have to reject his version.

"Let me stipulate something here and now. Mr. Myers felt that Mr. Burgess wronged him three years ago. Mr. Burgess lied, and it cost Mr. Myers more than a year of his life. Let me also stipulate that Mr. Myers was in Mr. Burgess's house at the moment he died, and that he entered through a window.

"You will hear why all of that does not add up to Chris Myers's guilt; not even close. Mr. Burgess, for all his faults and misdeeds, is an unfortunate victim here; he paid for his involvement in a scheme with his life. But Chris Myers is also a victim, trapped in a three-year nightmare, and we will show you exactly how that has transpired.

"Mr. Morrow gets to go first; he will present the state's case before we get a chance to present ours. I ask that you keep an open mind, that you understand even while you listen to him that there is another side to the story. When we get to show you that side, to offer you facts and witnesses to support it, I believe you will decide that Chris Myers has been victimized far too much already, and you will right that wrong.

"Thank you."

I sit down at the table, tapping Chris on the shoulder in a gesture of support. I told the jury that I basically would prove to them that Chris was framed. If I don't do that, if I don't deliver, then we are dead in the water. Juries don't like when you promise something and don't follow through.

If I can't deliver, then it doesn't matter whether they feel resentful or not . . . they will find Chris guilty anyway.

It's not like there are different levels of guilt; they can't find Chris *very* guilty, or *terribly* guilty.

Guilty is guilty.

W e call Sergeant Gail Wilhelm."

Morrow's first witness is a sergeant in the Forensics Division of the Paterson Police Department. She's far from the most senior member of the unit, but she has been there for five years and is quite competent. She's also a good witness, professional and unflappable.

Not that Morrow had a choice as to which person in the division to call; Wilhelm processed the murder scene at Burgess's house. She did the work, so she is the one to describe it and defend it.

After Morrow quickly takes her through her credentials, she confirms that she did the forensics work at Burgess's house.

"Did you find any open windows?"

"Yes, a side window that leads into the master bedroom was wide open."

"Did you test it for fingerprints?"

"Yes."

"Did you find any?"

"We did. There were prints on both the windowsill and the window itself."

Morrow introduces a photograph of the window and asks Wilhelm to show where the prints were found. "Is this consistent with where prints would be found if the window was being opened from the outside?"

"Yes."

"Did you match the prints to anyone?"

"Yes, the fingerprints are those of Christopher Myers."

"Thank you."

I have nothing to use to challenge what Wilhelm has said; the prints were certainly there. I also stipulated during my opening statement that Chris entered through the window. But I can make a few other points.

"Sergeant, the prints you found were clear and well preserved?"

"Yes."

"Is there a way to remove prints after one leaves them?"

"What do you mean?"

"Well, for example, if your prints are on the witness stand where you are sitting, as I assume they are, could you, say, wipe them off if you didn't want them there?"

"Of course."

"And that would prevent anyone from later proving you were there by your fingerprints?"

"Yes."

"But that wasn't done in this case? No wiping was done on the window?"

"No. The prints were clear."

"Did you check anywhere else in the house for prints?"

"Yes, certainly."

"Did you check the outside knob on the front door?"

"Yes."

"Were Mr. Myers's unwiped prints there as well?"

"Yes."

"So it's fair to assume that he tried to enter through the front door as well as the window?"

"I suppose so. I can't be sure."

"Well, if he left through the front door, he would have had no reason to touch the outside knob, would he?"

"Not necessarily."

"Were his prints on the inside front doorknob?"

"Yes."

"Did you examine the back door for prints?"

She nods. "Yes. There were none."

I feign surprise. "Really? Was it a new doorknob?"

"No, sir. Did not seem to be."

"But never been used? Since there were no prints?"

"I couldn't say."

"What about the inside back doorknob? Did you find any prints on that."

"There were no prints."

"Did that one appear to have been picked up from Home Depot that morning?"

Morrow objects and I rephrase, asking if it seemed new.

"It did not," Wilhelm says.

"Is it possible prints were wiped off the inside and outside back doorknobs?"

"I don't know."

"You don't know if it's possible?"

"Oh, sorry. It's definitely possible."

"Thank you. No further questions."

Morrow's next witness is the first officer on the scene, Patrolman Louis Myatt. A neighbor, the one who heard the shot and saw Chris run out of the house, called 911.

"Please describe what you found when you arrived."

"Well, the front door was open. We called out and got no response. Because of that, and the fact that an argument and a shot was reported as having been heard from inside the house, we felt we had justification to enter.

"Once we were inside, we saw Mr. Burgess lying on the floor in the den. He had an obvious bullet wound in the side of the head and was lying facedown. I checked his vital signs and confirmed that he was deceased, while my partner looked to see if anyone else was in the house.

"Once death was confirmed, I assisted my partner in going through the house. After that, we secured the scene and waited for Homicide to arrive."

"Did you reach any conclusions about how the perpetrator might have entered?"

"That wasn't our responsibility, but I did notice that a side window was open."

"Was the back door open?"

"It was slightly ajar."

Morrow turns the witness over to me. I have little to accomplish, and he did no damage to us, but I still don't want him to get off unscathed.

"Officer Myatt, you said the back door was slightly ajar."

"Yes."

"What exactly does that mean?"

"It was open about six inches, maybe more."

"So it's possible that someone could have come in through there and didn't close it fully when leaving?"

"I couldn't say."

"Yes, you could. You just don't want to."

Morrow objects, and Judge McVay sustains the objection and admonishes me.

"No further questions."

Judge McVay adjourns court for the day; it wasn't a good day, but it was better than the ones coming up.

A t least on the surface, Heyer is what he appears to be—a college professor who has attained a significant position in his field."

Corey has come back from Massachusetts, where he was learning what he could about Clifford Heyer, the MIT professor who spent ten days in the Hotel Metuska. Sam is here also; I've asked him to find out what he can about Heyer as well.

Corey continues, "The man is extremely well respected, regarded as one of the preeminent minds in the field of nuclear physics. Colleagues and students speak about him with a reverence; they consider him a genius, and I have no reason to doubt that.

"He's in his midforties, not married, and lives in a house about two blocks from campus, in Cambridge. His salary is two hundred and seventy thousand dollars a year, which he supplements by giving speeches to nerdy groups, mostly in the East."

"Wow . . . that's more than I thought professors get paid," Sam says.

"Sam, backup shortstops make five million," I say. "Go on, Corey."

"I followed him from his house to a bar about twelve

blocks away; he passed at least a half dozen other bars on the way, without stopping there. My assessment is that he went to this particular bar because it was well away from the campus and he was unlikely to be recognized.

"I entered after him and did not notice him greet or acknowledge any of the other patrons. He just went to the bar and started drinking; the bartender did not need to be told what to serve him, so he is obviously at least a semiregular.

"I sat next to him and tried a few times to strike up a conversation, but he had no interest in engaging. I believe he is nervous and under a lot of stress, but I am clearly not a psychiatrist. I do think he is a heavy drinker, but I have no way of knowing how long that has been going on, or whether or not he is capable of stopping."

"Interesting," I say.

"I haven't told you the bombshell yet. A couple of months ago an associate professor at MIT, also in nuclear physics, turned up dead in the Charles River with his neck broken. His name was Keith Richter, and he was a protégé of Clifford Heyer."

Laurie whistles. "Bombs away. Any chance arrests were made?"

"No. Case is currently open and unsolved."

"Can Heyer be rattled?" I ask.

"He's already rattled. Obviously I don't know why, but this guy seems on the edge. Won't take much to push him over."

"So let's push," I say. "Let's try and shake him. Sam, you have his number?"

"Yes."

"And you can track any calls he makes after I talk to him?"

"Of course."

"Okay, good. We'll take tonight and during the day tomorrow to figure out the best approach to take and make the call to him tomorrow night. If I call and he's not there, I don't want him to know that it was me who called. I don't want him at all prepared. So can you show me how to make my number show up as 'private caller'?"

"Duh. Anybody can do that."

"Trust me, Sam, not anybody. Also, I assume that Heyer has published a bunch of papers related to his field. Can you find them and print them out for me? I need them right away."

"Sure."

"Corey, I hate to ask this, but can you go back up to Cambridge?"

"Of course. Why?"

"I want to scare this guy, and if you're present and he knows it, that can be intimidating."

"I'll bring Simon."

"Good idea; Simon can be a hell of a lot scarier than you." I say this even though Simon is in the other room with Tara, Sebastian, and Hunter, and they're all peacefully sound asleep. "Okay, good, now everybody out of here. I need to make a call. Laurie, you can stay."

She laughs. "Thanks, Andy."

Once the others have left, I call Richard Wallace. I know he often works late at the prosecutor's offices, but I try him at home first.

He answers with "Hey, Andy. You're not pissed that

I told Morrow about our conversation, are you? The one about Burgess changing his mind about recanting?"

"I'm furious," I lie, and he knows I'm lying. "But I'm going to give you a chance to make up for it by doing something you've never done before."

"Uh-oh. I'm starting to think I should have screened this call."

"Too late now. I need to talk to you tomorrow before court. It's very important."

"Can you give me a preview now?"

"I'd rather not. But at the very least, you can look forward to an interesting conversation."

He laughs. "Andy, you are always interesting. But let's not meet at my office; my lawyers might think I'm a traitor and a defense sympathizer. I'd never get invited to another prosecution party."

"Fair enough. You pick the place. Oh, and keep tomorrow night open."

"Tomorrow night? This is an all-day request?"

"Could be."

We decide on a coffee shop about a mile from the courthouse. "See you tomorrow," I say. "I'll pick up the tab; all you have to do is bring an open mind."

He laughs again. "Where the hell am I going to get one of those?"

Richard is waiting for me when I arrive at the coffee shop.

He is early and I'm not because he doesn't have to wait while Sebastian walks along at a brisk speed of one mile per week, stopping occasionally to rest and piss.

I think it drives Tara even crazier than me. I wouldn't be shocked if one day she wrapped her paws around his chubby neck and strangled him. There's not a canine court in the country that would convict her.

Richard has gotten a table in the back, with no other customers around. He doesn't know what I'm going to say, but I'm pretty confident he doesn't want anyone else to hear it.

I've got to get to court soon, so I don't have a lot of time to chitchat. I get right to it. "I want to give you the rare opportunity to be a witness for the defense."

He smiles. "God forbid."

"I'm serious."

"I was afraid you were. Start from the beginning, please."

"I will. But first I need your word that you'll keep this conversation confidential. No regaling your colleagues with it around the watercooler."

"We don't have watercoolers anymore, but I won't repeat

it unless it violates my oath not to. I can't know for sure until I hear it."

I nod. "That works."

I tell him where we are in the case so far, focusing on what is going on in Metuska, but also including Paul Donnelly. It takes less than ten minutes because unfortunately we don't know much.

He listens carefully, without interrupting. I'm sure he's dying to know why I am sharing all this with him, but he's letting me get there at my own pace.

I eventually get to the MIT professor, Clifford Heyer, and my impending phone call with him. "That's where you come in. To start with, I want you to listen in on the call when I make it."

"Why?"

"Because, for one thing, I may need someone to testify to the truthfulness of it. I'm also going to tape it."

"What did you mean when you said you want me to listen in 'to start with'?"

"I think and hope it's going to shake things out, and I want you to be able to testify to the repercussions as well. We may never need you, especially if things don't turn out the way we want. But I'm hoping we do."

"To what do I owe this honor?"

"At the risk of flattering you, you're credible, and as a defense witness you're even more credible. The jury would believe you more than anyone else because of your position and reputation."

He thinks for a moment. "When I asked why you want me to do it, you said that 'for one thing' you might want me to testify. What's the other thing?"

"Wow, you hang on my every word, don't you?"

He smiles. "I've learned to be careful around you."

"There is also a chance that we may have to call in law enforcement, not here but in Pennsylvania, or maybe Massachusetts. They would be way more likely to respond to you than me. The Taliban would have more credibility with law enforcement than I would."

"Very true."

We're both silent for a while, while he thinks about the situation. This is a big ask; he knows it and I know it.

"I'd get a lot of pushback from my people for this," he says. "They wouldn't like it. The word *turncoat* would get thrown around a lot."

"We're supposed to be in a search for the truth, Richard. All you'd be doing is telling the truth."

"Not everybody will see it that way."

"There's one other thing. Whatever is going on is far from over. You could be preventing more murders, or other serious crimes."

"I don't want to be included in any strategy discussions. If I'm there, it's strictly as an observer."

"Agreed."

Another pause as he considers it. Finally, "Okay. I'm in."

I smile. "Thank you. And welcome to the defense team."

Henry Renteria is the neighbor who saw and heard Chris at the time of the Burgess shooting.

Morrow's calling him to the stand and, after having called forensics and the officers on the scene, makes it clear that he wants to deal with the facts of the shooting before moving on to motive.

Morrow quickly sets the scene, then asks Renteria to explain where he was at the time of the shooting.

"I was walking my dog. Mr. Burgess lived three houses down from me, and we were approaching his house."

Morrow shows a photograph of the neighborhood, taken from above. For all I know Corey's drone friend could have taken it. Morrow uses it to let Renteria show exactly where he was, which was one house down from Burgess's.

"Please describe what you saw and heard." I'm sure Morrow sees no danger in leaving the request open-ended, since they must have gone over this testimony repeatedly.

"Well, first I heard yelling, like loud arguing between two people."

"Did you recognize the voices?"

"I recognized Charlie's voice . . . Charlie Burgess. Not the other one."

"Could you understand what they were saying?"

"No, but I wasn't really trying to. It was none of my business. In our neighborhood, everybody believes in minding their own business."

"What happened next?"

"I heard a gunshot. It sounded like it came from inside Charlie's house."

"Are you familiar with the sound of a gunshot?"

"Oh, yes. I'm a member of a rifle club, and I'm licensed to own firearms. I have two pistols and a rifle. So I'm very familiar with the sound."

"What did you do after you heard the shot?"

"Well, I really didn't have time to do anything. A man came running out the front door; he looked either scared or upset or something. He ran to his car, which was parked in front of Charlie's house, and drove away. It all happened really quickly."

"Did he close the door to Mr. Burgess's house behind him?"

"No."

"Did you get his license plate number?"

"Yes, I thought it could be important."

"What did you do next?"

"Well, I didn't have my cell phone with me, so I went home and called nine-one-one. I also wrote down the license plate number, so I wouldn't forget it."

"And the police arrived quickly?"

"Oh, yes. The cops were there in just a couple of minutes; I met them outside and told them what happened. I also gave them the license plate number on the man's car.

"They told me to wait in the squad car, and then after a

while another group of police cars showed up, at least five. They questioned me, I signed a statement, and that was it."

"Who was the man who came running out of Mr. Burgess's house, after the shot was fired?"

"He was"—Renteria points—"Mr. Myers."

"Are you certain about that?"

"Absolutely."

Morrow turns the "absolutely certain" witness over to me.

"Mr. Renteria, you said that the man was parked directly in front of Mr. Burgess's house?"

"Yes."

"If he wanted to, could he have parked some place where his car would not have been seen?"

"What do you mean?"

I show on the photograph the place behind the house where I suspect the real killer parked. "If he had parked here, could he have approached the house from the back this way?"

"Yes, I guess so."

"Did you know the back door was open when the police arrived?"

"No, I didn't. I was in the front."

"Did the man make any effort to hide when he came out? For example, did he shield his face?"

Renteria shakes his head. "No. I saw him clearly."

"He didn't look around for witnesses?"

"No."

"Do you think he saw you?"

"He should have. I was right there. I don't know how he could have missed me."

"Did he shoot at you? To keep you quiet?"

Another firm shake of the head. "No."

"Did you see a gun?"

"A gun?"

"Yes, the thing he would have had to have in order to have shot Mr. Burgess. Did you see it?"

"No."

"So a frightened-looking man came out, in plain sight through the front door, rather than the window, making no effort to conceal himself. He was not holding a gun, and he ran to his car, which was parked directly in front of the house where the murder was committed. Is that your testimony?"

Renteria thinks for a moment. "Yes, it is."

I let him off the stand. I didn't exactly land any bombshells, but I had none to land. Renteria has just buried Chris in the eyes of the jury, and I did little to change that.

During the lunch hour, Corey calls to tell me that he is in place. He will follow Heyer when he leaves the campus. Not too close, but close enough to make sure that Heyer sees him and Simon.

He doubts that Heyer will recognize him, since Heyer had been drinking heavily in the bar the night Corey tried to strike up a conversation.

If Heyer repeats his actions from that night, he will go home before heading to the bar. If he does that, Corey will notify me when he's there, so I can call. I definitely want to catch him sober.

I call Richard and tell him to come by the house around 6:00 P.M.

"I should not be doing this," he says.

"Search for the truth, Richard. Search for the truth. You're on the right side of this."

"I'm not on any side."

"Good enough."

Morrow spends the afternoon session questioning the arresting officer, Lieutenant Mike Scharf. He led a group of six cops to Chris's house, read him his rights, and took him into custody.

When asked how he came to suspect Chris, he mentions

Renteria and the license plate number. "I ran the plate, then made some calls and found out about an obvious motive."

"You came to understand that Mr. Myers had a grudge against Mr. Burgess?"

"Yes, sir."

Morrow makes no attempt to have Scharf explain the motive at this point, and I don't press it on cross-examination. That fight will be further down the road, meaning tomorrow.

For now, that there is a motive has been planted in the jury's minds, and they can refer back to Morrow's opening statement, when he briefly described it.

As is becoming a pattern, I have little ammunition to use on the witness. "Lieutenant Scharf, how much time passed from the time you arrived on the scene to the time you went to Mr. Myers's house and made the arrest?"

"Just over three hours."

"Did you first call Mr. Renteria in to physically and personally identify Mr. Myers and confirm that he was the man he saw?"

"No."

"You just went by the license plate?"

"And the motive."

"What if Mr. Myers had lent somebody his car? Or if it had been stolen?"

"The car was there when we arrived at the defendant's house."

I frown my disdain for this answer. "What if he had lent the car to someone who committed the crime and then returned the car? How could you have known that had not happened?"

"I believe we had probable cause to make the arrest."

"Did you find Mr. Myers's prints on the murder weapon?"

"We did not recover a murder weapon."

"Really? Did you remember to search Mr. Myers's house and car, or would that have moved the investigation past the three-hour mark?"

Morrow objects that I am badgering. McVay sustains the objection, warns me, and tells me to rephrase the question. I do that, leaving out the snide part at the end.

"We searched the house and car, but there were plenty of places for him to have gotten rid of the gun on the route home."

"So the Mets can't finish a game in under three hours, but that's all the time you need to conduct a sufficient murder investigation?"

"To make the arrest? Yes. And it turns out I was right."

"I've got an idea, Lieutenant Scharf. How about if we let the jury decide if you were right?"

Judge McVay adjourns for the day, rather than start a new witness that we might not be able to finish. I'm pleased by that because I want to prepare for my call with Clifford Heyer.

That will be more important than anything that happened in court today.

What are we hoping will come out of this?" Laurie asks.

"In a perfect world?" I ask. "That we scare him enough that he turns on Fulton and Donnelly and tells what he knows to the police."

"Seems unlikely."

"Probably, but definitely not impossible. Failing that, we frighten him into making a mistake, maybe revealing something about the conspiracy."

Richard is not here yet, but should be in a few minutes. We're also waiting for Corey's call telling us that Heyer is in his house. It's possible that his routine will be different tonight, and he won't go home until after a trip to the bar. In that case, we will probably abort and place the call tomorrow.

Laurie had taken Ricky to his friend Will Rubenstein's house for a sleepover. We do not want Ricky listening to this stuff when we can avoid it. Unfortunately, we can't always avoid it.

Richard arrives, greeting Laurie with a big hug. She leads him into the kitchen, where he starts in enthusiastically on the pizzas we brought in for dinner. If he's nervous and uncertain about what he's doing, he's hiding it well. I'm the one who's nervous, knowing that as soon as Corey makes the call, if he does, that I will be center stage.

The phone rings, and the sound seems extraloud as it echoes through the house. I look at the caller ID and say, "Telemarketer." I'm usually glad about that, but tonight I'm not. I want to get this over with.

Twenty minutes later the phone rings again, and this time it's Corey. "He's left the campus. I made sure he saw me, but I don't think it registered."

"It will. Is he headed home?"

"He's going in that direction, but I can't be certain. I'll call you back."

We're all set. Sam is tapped into my phone and will record the call, which is legal, since Jersey is a one-party-consent state. I have not told Richard that Sam will be tracking Heyer's calls through the phone company computers after Heyer gets off the phone with me. It's illegal, and I don't want to put Richard or Sam in that position.

Fifteen minutes later, Corey calls back. "He just entered his house. Simon and I are moving into position now."

"Okay. I'll give it five minutes."

I wait the five minutes, which feel like five days. When the time is up, I call Heyer's phone, with our own phone set to show PRIVATE CALLER. Richard picks up the extension once Heyer's phone rings.

There is the danger that Heyer hates talking on the phone as much as I do and will screen the call.

He doesn't. He answers with "Hello" on the second ring.

"Professor Heyer, my name is Andy Carpenter. I am an attorney and an officer of the court."

"I'm sorry, I don't have—"

"Professor, I know what is going on in Metuska."

He doesn't answer; I hope that is because he is stunned and feeling some level of panic.

"I am now informing you that this phone call is your one and only chance to extricate yourself from this situation in a way that doesn't end up with you in prison, or worse."

"I have nothing to say." I can hear the nervousness in his voice.

"You don't have to say anything; for now you can just listen. We know about Metuska and Samuel Fulton and Paul Donnelly and all that you are doing there."

There is a long pause. "That was terrible about Mr. Donnelly." It's a strange way for him to describe a murderer; I wonder if Heyer is all that mentally stable. Or maybe he started his drinking tonight at home.

"It is about to come crashing down on all of them. Your choice is a simple one. You can go down with them, or cooperate and save yourself."

"Save myself? You don't know them. You don't know what they are like."

"Oh, but I do, and so do the authorities. Professor, I want you to look out your window. There is a man out there, with a German shepherd. That is his police dog. I'll hold on."

I can hear him put the phone down, and after about twenty seconds he comes back. "I see them."

"His name is Corey Douglas. He is staying at the Double-Tree, right there in Cambridge. If you decide to cooperate, you should call him there and he will provide protection and bring you to the authorities.

"If you decide not to cooperate, you can expect to be arrested and jailed very soon. It's your choice, and you have until tomorrow to make it."

"What we are doing in Metuska is not illegal," he says, jarring me.

Richard looks at me, eyebrows raised, also not understanding the comment.

"Murder is illegal," I say. "Try making that argument to your colleague Professor Richter, and the others. You will go down for conspiracy to commit serial murder, Professor." I'm a bit out of my comfort zone here; I don't have any certainty that Richter, whose body turned up in the Charles River, was a victim of this conspiracy. But I'm betting he was.

"When this started, I did not know they would do these terrible things. But they'll kill me; they can get to anyone."

"You have one chance, Professor, and that is Corey Douglas at the DoubleTree Hotel. You can get your life back, or you can go down with the rest of them."

"I have to think."

"Think hard." I hang up.

Richard hangs up as well, then turns to me. "Holy shit."

"Well put. What do you think he will do?"

"You told him you know what's going on. Do you?"

"No."

"If it's nuclear, could they be making a bomb? Maybe hold a city for ransom?"

"I don't think so, but we will have to call in the Feds if we don't rule that out soon."

"He said that what they are doing is not illegal."

I nod. "I know. I don't understand that. Why would you commit multiple murders to protect something legal? And if he believes I know what is happening, why bother lying and saying it's legal? They might have somehow sold him a load of bullshit, and he bought it."

"Okay. You've convinced me; that was not a guy who is doing the right thing. No matter what it is, and no matter what his reason. I'm here when you need me."

"Thanks, Richard. I'm not surprised."

Richard leaves and I immediately call Sam. "Well?" is all I ask.

"He called Fulton. They talked for seven minutes."

I'm a little disappointed to hear this. It further confirms that Heyer is knee-deep in this, but we knew that already. My concern is that if he called Fulton, it could mean that he is sticking with him, and they are trying to figure a way out of the problem that I present.

I call Corey and update him on what went on, and he promises to stay at the hotel as long as needed. He'll get room service for him and Simon, and the only time he will leave the room is to take Simon for his bathroom walks. Fortunately, Simon is not Sebastian, so they will be quick.

Meanwhile, I settle in to read Heyer's published works. Nothing like spending a night reading a bunch of physics papers that I completely do not understand.

Should be fun.

Today should be the last day of the prosecution's case, and it will be all about motive.

The situation for us is far worse than just the jury learning that Chris had reason to have a grudge against Burgess. They will also learn that he was in jail previously for killing a man.

That it was involuntary manslaughter will for them be a distinction without a difference. It's human nature for them to think that if he could kill once, he could kill again. It's my fault for putting humans on the jury.

Morrow's first witness is a retired cop, Luther Davis, who was a lieutenant in the Homicide Division of the Paterson Police Department for twenty-six years. Even though Chris wasn't ultimately charged with homicide, that was a later prosecutorial decision, so Homicide is the division that handled it.

Morrow takes him through his impressive career, and Davis comes off as modest and affable. When I question him, his persona will change. I've had him on the stand a bunch of times over the years, and he can be an obnoxious pain in the ass to cross-examine.

"Lieutenant Davis, you were in charge of a case involving the defendant, Mr. Myers, almost three years ago?"

"Yes." Davis doesn't bother to correct Morrow by saying he is retired and no longer a lieutenant. I don't object either; there's no upside to doing so.

"Can you describe that case to the jury?"

"There was a fight in the alley behind a place called the Basement Bar in downtown Paterson. The participants were Mr. Myers and a man named Joseph Bonaventura. Mr. Bonaventura was killed, and the cause of death was a fractured skull. The coroner ruled that death was the result of his being knocked unconscious and hitting the back of his head on the pavement when he fell."

"Mr. Myers threw the punch?"

"Yes."

"Were there witnesses?"

"The bartender was a witness to an argument between the two men before they went out back to settle it. Then there was an actual eyewitness to the fight."

"Who was the eyewitness?"

"Charles Burgess."

Morrow pauses for a moment to let that sink in for the jury. Then, "Lieutenant, would you have secured a conviction if Mr. Burgess had not witnessed the event and testified about it?"

"I am not an expert about what might have happened in the trial, but I can confidently say that without Mr. Burgess, we wouldn't even have made an arrest."

"Thank you, no further questions."

I stand and immediately start to fire questions. "Mr. Davis, you said that without Mr. Burgess's testimony, you would not have made an arrest. Does that mean you did not have DNA evidence?"

"We did not."

"Even though Mr. Myers allegedly punched him hard enough to cause unconsciousness?"

"It happens."

"I see. What about in the bruises on Mr. Myers's hands? Was Mr. Bonaventura's DNA found on them?"

"We did not find bruises on Mr. Myers's hands."

"Is your explanation for that the same? 'It happens'?"

"Yes." I can see that Davis is getting annoyed with me. Breaks my heart.

"So this obviously immaculate fight was witnessed only by Mr. Burgess?"

"He was the only eyewitness that came forward."

"That's convenient. Did you investigate Mr. Burgess's situation at the time?"

"What do you mean?"

"Well, for instance, were you aware that he was a compulsive gambler?"

"There were rumors to that effect."

I introduce three sworn affidavits that Laurie got from three of Burgess's friends attesting to his gambling habit and show them to Davis.

"This makes it more than rumor, doesn't it?"

"Gamblers can be witnesses."

"Was Mr. Burgess working at the time?"

"No, he had left his job at the post office six months earlier."

"How did he pay his gambling debts?"

"I don't know."

"Is it possible he was paid to lie about the fight and then used the money to pay off the debts?"

"We found no evidence of that."

"We have some time, Mr. Davis. Tell us what you did to determine where Mr. Burgess got his money. How exactly did you come to understand that Mr. Burgess was not paid to lie?"

"It's impossible to prove a negative." This is close to a non sequitur. "We found nothing that raised suspicions."

"I see. Let's turn to the victim, then, Mr. Bonaventura." I introduce evidence to support what Sam found, that there is no trace of Bonaventura for more than the past six months of his life. Eddie had subpoenaed the records legally, so we don't have to use Sam's less than legal versions.

"Does this surprise you, Mr. Davis?"

"I would have to look more carefully at it . . . study it."

"Did you run Mr. Bonaventura's DNA?"

"Of course."

"Did you get a match?"

"No, but that only means he was never arrested or in the armed forces."

"Did you try to locate next of kin?"

"We did, but were unsuccessful."

"Are you aware of anyone reporting him missing at that time? Any missing person reports, or reports of him leaving suddenly?" As I'm asking the question, a realization hits me that is so jarring I almost lose my train of thought.

"No."

"Your Honor, I have another area of questioning for Mr. Davis that might take us past the end of the court day. I would request that we adjourn now and I can finish questioning Mr. Davis in the morning."

Judge McVay agrees, and court is adjourned.

When I get home, I ask Laurie to scan a picture from the discovery of Bonaventura into my computer. She and Ricky are the only two humans living at our house that are capable of scanning something.

She does so, and I call Denise Holman. "Denise, I just emailed you a photograph. I'm afraid it is of a person who is deceased, but that's all I have. Please tell me if you recognize it."

"Okay, hold on, let me open my iPad."

I wait for a while.

"Here it is. . . . I'm opening it." Then, "Oh my God . . . it's Alex Swain."

I let that sink in for a few moments. "Denise, I need you to do something for me . . . and for Alex."

Alex Swain did not run off with the hard-earned money of the homeowners of Metuska.

He was likely kidnapped and then killed as part of a process to set up Chris Myers. It removed two dangers to the operation at one time, eliminating both the lawyer and the client. It allowed whatever is going on in Metuska to continue unimpeded.

This revelation represents a huge opportunity for our defense, if we can present this information to our advantage. It casts doubt on the entire investigation of the Bonaventura (now Swain) killing, and therefore casts doubt on whether Burgess witnessed it as he said he did.

And if he didn't witness it, if he lied, then the claim that he was paid to lie becomes credible. Everything flows from that.

I wish I had thought earlier of the possibility that the victim was really Swain. Chris had never met Swain, so it makes sense that he didn't know what he looked like and didn't recognize him in the crime-scene photos.

I spend some more time this evening going through papers on nuclear physics that Heyer has written. I understand every third or fourth word; I feel like I could use subtitles in plain English.

I take a welcome break and tuck Ricky into bed. We talk some baseball and some Superman. Right now I wish I could be the lawyer version of Superman. I could go into a phone booth, if any still existed, whip off my glasses, and become . . . Clarence Darrow.

Tomorrow is a big day in court, so I want to be well rested. I head for bed around ten o'clock; Laurie is already asleep.

We are getting old.

The alarm clock wakes me, or at least that's what I think is happening until I realize that we don't have an alarm clock. As I'm starting to process this, I hear Laurie say, "I'm on it."

I look over, and she is putting down her cell phone. I look at my own cell phone on the night table and it says 1:48.

This is not good.

"What's going on?" I say it softly, almost in a whisper, because some instinct tells me that's what I should do. "Who was that?"

Laurie is already getting out of bed. She talks even more softly than I did. "Andy, that was Marcus. Go into Ricky's room, close the door, and make sure he does not come out. . . . Stay in there with him . . . no matter what."

"What's going on?"

"Andy, please just do it now. We have visitors."

So I do it. I know that Laurie is shielding me and Ricky from an obvious danger, but this is no time to argue the point. In our house, unlike on the *Titanic*, we don't protect the women and children first. Here it's the lawyers and children that have the first crack at the lifeboats.

I go into Ricky's room and leave the door ajar slightly so I can hear what is going on. For three minutes that feel like at least a decade, I hear nothing.

Then I hear a loud thumping noise and Laurie yell, *"Freeze, asshole!"*

She can be charming when she wants to be.

The next sound is bone-chilling; it's a gunshot.

I simply cannot stay in this room any longer. I open the door and leave, closing it behind me. Ricky has slept through the whole thing, at least so far, which is lucky for us.

I head toward the stairway and hear another thud and then the front door opening. I move forward some more and see Marcus throw a large man into the foyer. I think the previous thud must have been Marcus using the guy's head as a battering ram to try to open the door.

The guy is bleeding from the head and seemingly unconscious, so I guess the door won and the ram lost. He also had the disadvantage of not having any hair on his head to cushion the crash; either his head is shaved or he's just completely bald.

The bookmaker, Dinardo, had said that one of the tough guys who came to ask him about Burgess had a shaved head. This might be a different guy, obviously, but that's not the way I'd bet.

Laurie comes in from the back area of the house with another large human walking in front of her. He is bleeding from the right shoulder and holding on to it with his left hand, as his right arm hangs loosely at his side.

"Is it just these two?" I say.

"Just these two," Laurie says. "Call nine-one-one."

I go to the phone, but instead of calling nine-one-one, I call Richard Wallace at home. He answers the phone in a groggy voice, which makes a lot of sense, considering the time.

"Richard, it's Andy. I need you to come over to the house right away."

"Andy . . . it's the middle of the night."

"I am aware of that. Please come over; I'm about to call nine-one-one."

"What happened?"

"It can be a surprise for when you get here."

Before I actually call the police, I open Ricky's door and check on him. He's still sound asleep, so I close the door again and make the call.

The cops get here before Richard does, but only by about five minutes. They're still listening to our explanations of what happened when he gets here, and I take him into the kitchen and give him the abridged version.

"Why am I here?" he asks when I'm done.

"A, because you can more credibly testify to what you personally witness."

"Andy . . ."

"And B, so you can run these guys through your superduper computers. You might be able to hopefully tie them to Paul Donnelly's operation, and that is something that the jury will find interesting."

"Any chance I can resign from the defense team?"

"Nope, it's a lifetime appointment."

"Where were you when Marcus knocked one of them out and Laurie shot the other one?"

"Sorry, that's on a need-to-know basis. Only the top members of the team are privy to that information."

He nods. "That's what I figured. You were hiding under the bed."

"Close enough."

Denise Holman arrived in New Jersey last night at about eleven o'clock.

We got her a room at a hotel in Paramus; it's lucky we didn't put her up at our house; it's not nice to have guests over to witness a shooting.

Eddie picked her up early this morning, helped her prepare the document, and being a notary himself, he took care of that as well. Eddie and Denise are waiting for me at the courthouse when I arrive.

"I heard you had some excitement last night," Eddie says. "You made the morning news and all the papers."

"Just another day at the office."

I thank Denise for coming. She's still shaken up about the news that Alex Swain was killed, but this is a tough lady. Before we have more than a minute or so to talk, Judge McVay comes in and the day's session begins.

Both the judge and Morrow express concern for my well-being, but I don't make much of it. I probably will later, but this is not the time.

Retired lieutenant Luther Davis takes the stand, prepared for round two. He's not going to like it.

"Mr. Davis, yesterday we were talking about the involuntary manslaughter conviction of Mr. Myers, and I was asking you how carefully you checked into the victim's background. Do you remember that?"

"Of course."

"And I showed you evidence that Mr. Bonaventura had at best a strangely skimpy background, and you said that a DNA check turned up nothing and that you could not find next of kin. Remember that as well?"

"Yes."

"Can I assume that you think your investigation was sufficient?"

"I do."

"What if I were to tell you that Joseph Bonaventura was not even Joseph Bonaventura?"

"I don't know what you mean."

I introduce Denise's signed affidavit and say that she is here to testify if necessary. I also show a few photographs that Denise had of Swain from community gatherings, and some google images of him. It is clear that Bonaventura and Alex Swain are one and the same person.

Once that is done, I ask, "Do you still think your investigation was sufficient?"

"This is information that we did not have."

"Isn't the purpose of an investigation to uncover information that you don't have?"

He doesn't answer.

"How can you be sure you identified the correct perpetrator when you couldn't even get the victim right?"

Morrow objects, but before Judge McVay can rule on it, "I say, never mind, I withdraw the question." Then, "Mr. Davis, now that we've established that you didn't know the correct identity of the victim, let's talk about where he died. I assume you think it was in the alley behind the bar?"

"Yes."

"How do you know that?"

"We had a witness."

I nod. "Right. Mr. Burgess, the only man who could have recanted and cleared Mr. Myers. Yet Mr. Myers is accused of killing him, thereby removing any possibility of being cleared. That's the Mr. Burgess you're talking about?"

Morrow objects that I am making an argument rather than questioning the witness. Since he's right about that, Judge McVay sustains the objection and tells the reporter to strike my remark from the record.

"Could Mr. Swain have been kidnapped from Metuska and brought to the alley that night, already deceased, with his head already crushed?"

"No."

"Why not? Was there a dent in the cement alley?"

"The coroner ruled he was killed there," Davis says, clearly annoyed.

"No, the coroner ruled Mr. Bonaventura was killed there. We've now proven that Mr. Bonaventura never even existed. Isn't it possible that this new information, which the coroner did not have, might be relevant?"

"We had a witness, and the bartender saw them go into the back alley."

"Is it possible the witnesses were paid to lie? And is it possible that when Mr. Burgess was thinking of recanting, he was killed to prevent it? If these people could kidnap Mr. Swain, could they not also murder him? Does that seem like a stretch to you?"

"We don't know that Swain was kidnapped."

"Right. Swain left Metuska, Pennsylvania, on his own and then just happened to show up behind the bar in Paterson, New Jersey, where his New York lawyer was drinking. Does that make sense to you, Mr. Davis?"

"I can't answer that at this point."

"Or does it make more sense that the witnesses were paid to lie?"

"There is no evidence of that."

"Maybe you should conduct an investigation. And maybe after that, you can give Mr. Myers the last three years of his life back."

Morrow is objecting, but I have already said, "No further questions."

Davis leaves the stand and Morrow calls three successive witnesses, all of whom have had conversations with Chris over the years, and all of whom say that he had expressed an anger at Burgess over his testimony in the Bonaventura . . . now Swain . . . case.

My questions for them are brief. I can't challenge them on any substantive ground, since Chris did have a grudge against Burgess and wasn't shy about saying so.

Morrow's final witness is a court clerk who testifies about our motion to appeal the conviction based on Burgess's promise to recant, and then our withdrawing the motion when he changed his mind.

It's an effective argument, since it presents a reason for a long-simmering grudge to come to a boil.

Then comes the line from Morrow that I've been dreading: "Your Honor, the prosecution rests."

I t feels like much about this case, and about our strategy, is a double-edged sword.

A perfect example is the revelation that Bonaventura was in fact Alex Swain. It was the kind of courtroom moment that defense attorneys live for, but it also came with a big negative.

It calls into question, at least to a degree, whether Chris's conviction the first time was fair. That's a positive for us—the bias against Chris that the jury must feel in believing that he killed before would be removed.

But if the jury comes to believe that Chris was wrongly convicted in Bonaventura's death, and that Burgess lied, that would intensify Chris's reason for holding a grudge. Burgess would have been responsible for unfairly taking away more than a year of Chris's life, and branding him a felon forever.

And what about the crime he's on trial for now . . . Burgess's murder? Just because Chris's outrage was legitimate, and Burgess perjured himself on the stand, Chris is still not free to murder him. Committing a homicide against a liar is just as serious an offense as committing one against a truthful person.

We seem to be getting nowhere with Clifford Heyer.

He has not called Fulton again, and since Sam is monitoring the GPS on his phone, we're pretty sure he has not left his house. Corey called the school and asked to speak with him and was told, "Professor Heyer is not in today."

I assume the attempt to invade our home the other night was Donnelly's reaction to my phone call to Heyer. If there is no other reaction, then my fear is that Heyer couldn't convince them that I know what is going on. Or maybe I didn't convince Heyer.

But the wheels of justice grind on, and we have to mount a defense. It's getting late in the court day, and Judge McVay asks me if I want to call a witness or wait. Court will not be in session tomorrow because the judge has other things on her docket that she has to deal with.

So I tell her that I want to call Denise Holman. I want to set up Metuska in the jurors' minds as a factor in this trial and drive home even more powerfully the fact that Joey Bonaventura was not Joey Bonaventura. Also, it's not fair to make Denise hang around; this way she can testify and go home.

Before that revelation about Bonaventura's real identity, Morrow could have fought anything at all about Metuska being admitted into evidence. He would have argued that it was out of left field, a fishing expedition with no apparent connection to the matter before our jury. Denise Holman would not even have been allowed to testify.

But revealing Bonaventura to be Swain changed all that. Not only does Swain bring Metuska into the picture, but by Morrow opening the door by bringing up the previous death in the first place, I have a lane to drive through.

On the witness stand, Denise Holman comes off as

nervous, but sincere. That's because she is nervous and sincere. I take her through a brief history of Metuska the last few years, talking about how the Fellows came in and then the town started buying up the land.

It takes a while, longer than I'd like, and I'm afraid I might be losing the jury. Then she gets to the point where Alex Swain rallied the homeowners and raised money to hire a law firm from New York that had experience in this area.

"The firm was Everson, Manning, and Winkler?"

"Yes."

"How did your group come to hire them?"

"Alex said they heard about our situation and came to us."

She talks about meeting Chris, and how he seemed anxious to help. Then all of a sudden the forward momentum on the case stopped. "Alex was gone, and we were told he must have sold his house without telling us and then took off with our money."

"And you stopped seeing Chris Myers?"

"Yes, a man named Caruso from the firm said he was assigned to the case. But we had no money, so I guess the firm dropped us. People just seemed to give up then, and a lot of them took the buyout money and moved out of Metuska."

I've debated whether to talk much about the specifics of the Fellows religion with Denise, but have decided against it. First of all, she knows little about it; they're secretive. But also, I don't want to risk offending any jurors who might be sensitive about the matter. The risk is not worth the reward.

Instead I have her mention the religion, and Fulton, and how they have come to dominate the community. I also have her talk about the lack of progress in the municipal improvements they are alleged to be doing.

Wrapping it up, I bring her back to Swain. "So you never saw Alex Swain again?"

She shakes her head sadly, fighting back tears that seem real. "Not alive. He was in that photograph you sent me. There's no question about it."

I turn her over to Morrow and sit back down at the defense table. As I do, Chris leans over and talks softly. "Andy, for what it's worth, we didn't approach Metuska to get them as a client."

"How did it happen?"

"I'm really not sure, but we would never have done that. They must have come to us."

"If you had approached them, who would have been the one that could do that?"

Chris thinks for a moment. "It would have to be Vic Everson."

"That's what I thought."

"But he never mentioned doing that."

"I'm not surprised." I've thought all along that it was unlikely the townspeople of Metuska would have picked a Manhattan law firm or even known about one. There are plenty of lawyers between Metuska and Central Park South.

Morrow's first question for Denise is about Swain; Morrow clearly believes, correctly, that at this point it's the only area of her testimony that can damage the prosecution.

"Ms. Holman, Alex Swain was a close friend of yours?"

"I thought so, yes."

"Until yesterday, when you saw his photo, you assumed he was alive?"

She nods. "Yes. I had no reason not to."

"And you believed that he had taken off with your money and the money of the other neighbors?"

"Yes."

"Did you try to find him?"

"We did for a while and then gave up."

"Ms. Holman, if someone embezzles money from his friends and neighbors and leaves town, would you be surprised to hear they might have assumed a different identity, so they would not be found?"

"I haven't thought about that."

"I understand. Please think about it now. Is it possible that Alex Swain took an assumed name so that he would not be found and possibly arrested? And that he just happened to get into a fight behind a bar after that?"

"It's possible, I suppose, but—"

"Thank you, Ms. Holman."

I wasn't going to ask any questions on redirect, but I decide to take a chance. "Ms. Holman, Mr. Morrow asked you if it was possible that Alex took on a different name and then got into a fight behind a bar. You said it was possible, and then you said 'but' before Mr. Morrow cut you off. Please finish your answer. 'But' what?"

"But Alex didn't drink . . . ever. Why would he be at a bar?"

Dinner is just ending when the dreaded phone rings. Caller ID says MYERS, which is a bit confusing since I know they haven't installed a private line in Chris's cell.

But since answering the call is the only way for me to clear up the confusion, I do so.

"Mr. Carpenter? It's Jessica Myers."

"Hello, Jessica" is my witty retort.

"I'm sorry to bother you at home."

"Just don't tell Paul Donnelly we talked. He'll yell at me again and send me to my room without supper. Or he might try and have me killed again, which is even worse."

"That's why I'm calling. I read about what happened last night, and I just wanted to say how sorry I am. I feel like I caused all of this. I never should have told Paul that we spoke."

"Don't worry about it, Jessica. It has nothing to do with you. It goes much deeper."

"Oh. Well, I don't know if I should be glad or sorry to hear that. But he's very protective of me . . . strangely so. I mean, I know the things he does and the type of man he is, but he has changed since Paul died."

I don't know how true that is, so I don't respond. Maybe the guy has changed on some emotional level and become less rational, but we're just talking about various degrees of awful.

"It's so hard to imagine them as father and son. They are so different. Paul could never do any of the things his father has done; he was so into beauty and love. Precious stones, art . . . he lived for those things."

I would ordinarily gag at the things that Jessica is saying, but not this time, because she just made me think of something. I want to get off the phone and think some more.

"Jessica, thank you for calling. But believe me, you have not caused me any problems. Maybe the opposite."

"What do you mean?"

"Long story; I'll have to tell you some other time."

I hang up and start to process what I've just realized; it may be real or it may be just another ridiculous idea to discard. First I want to discuss it with Laurie, and then I have to go back and reread one of the physics papers that Clifford Heyer wrote.

Then I have to remember a *Superman* episode that Ricky and I watched a few weeks ago.

But it's all going to have to wait because I have to call Eddie and tell him to get the judge to issue a subpoena for Vic Everson to testify. He might come in voluntarily, but I don't want to argue the point. I want him as fast as possible.

"Get him as early as you can, or it might have to wait until after work. He lives in Alpine, but his office is in the city, so that would complicate matters."

Eddie says he'll get on it immediately, and I no sooner hang up than the damn phone rings again. This time it's Corey Douglas.

"Clifford Heyer is gone," he says instead of "Hello."

"Gone where? Gone how?"

"I don't know where, but if I had to guess it would be Metuska. And as far as how, I don't think he went willingly."

"Why do you say that?"

"Because I went to his house with Simon. I figured we could take another shot at intimidating him, since we seemed to be getting nowhere. The door was open and he wasn't answering the bell, and I had a bad feeling about it, so I went in.

"There was food on the table, dried out, like it had been there for a while. A chair in the kitchen was turned over. He did not leave on his own; I'd bet anything on it."

"Okay. Call nine-one-one anonymously; just say you think Clifford Heyer was kidnapped. Don't give them any more information; they can take it from there. I just want to get the report in."

I hang up and call Richard Wallace.

"Uh-oh, what is it this time? I'm starting to hate the telephone."

"Join the club. Can you come over first thing in the morning, Richard? It's showtime."

"I'll be there."

We hang up. I want to talk to Laurie, and I want to process my thoughts. I also want to tear the phone out of the goddamn wall.

Richard is at the house at 8:00 A.M., and he's not here just to listen. He has news.

"This is not me being part of the defense team," he says, always anxious to make that clear. "But I've just heard something you will be interested in. Victor Everson was murdered last night."

This news hits me like the proverbial ton of bricks. "Tell me more."

"He got home from dinner, parked his car, and never made it into his house. One shot in the back of the head, execution-style."

"They're getting rid of everybody in any way involved who could hurt them." That doesn't at all change my view of what is going on; if anything, it solidifies it.

I ask Richard to wait a moment while I call Eddie and tell him to forget the subpoena. Whatever we were going to get from Everson on the stand, we'll have to get another way.

"Clifford Heyer was kidnapped," I tell Richard. "He's been gone at least thirty-six hours."

"Do you think he's dead?"

"No, I think they need him. When they don't need him anymore, he'll be dead a minute later."

"So you think he's in Metuska?"

"I don't think there's any question about it. That's why I asked you to come here. And I've got great news; you're going to be there tonight as well."

He does a double take. "How is that?"

"I need you to trigger an operation to save Heyer. We can credibly claim that he is a kidnapping victim, and you, because of your position, can attest that there is probable cause he is being held in Metuska."

"It's in Pennsylvania; I'm a prosecutor in New Jersey."

"I know that; which is why I will pave the way for you. I have a captain in the Pennsylvania State Police to contact who will be delighted to take Metuska apart. His name is Roger McKenny; I'll contact him and bring him up to speed.

"Corey and Simon will be there and will go in with you. That will be part of the deal we'll make with McKenny. But there's one other thing that will be crucial."

"What's that?"

"He has to keep a lid on it for twelve hours. It can't get into the media."

"Why?"

"Because I have more to worry about than nailing Fulton and Donnelly. I have to get all this in front of a jury, so I need to play it just right."

"Will McKenny buy into keeping it a secret?"

"He'll have to, or we'll threaten to go to the Feds with it. Heyer was taken from Massachusetts to Pennsylvania, across state lines. McKenny will not want to watch the Feds take over this operation. Oh, and tell him that while it's a secret, I want Heyer here. You can arrange custody."

While Richard is processing all this, I ask him to wait for a few minutes, and I call Harold Caruso at the office. While I expected to leave a message, he's in already and takes my call.

"You heard about Vic?" He sounds shell-shocked.

"I did."

"Is this about Metuska?"

"No question about it. They're getting rid of everyone who knows what is going on."

"I don't understand. . . . What did Vic know?"

"He was part of it. He approached Swain and took on the townspeople as clients, knowing he could sabotage it. I need your help."

"What can I do?"

"I need you to testify."

"About what?"

"About Metuska, about Fulton, about the Fellows . . . just whatever you know."

"I don't know much."

"I understand. I just need to paint a picture and a history of that place for the jury, and you can help. Chris needs your help."

"Okay. I'm in. But what the hell is going on in Metuska? It's a nothing town."

"It will all be clear tomorrow. But in the meantime, be careful. They may think you know more than you do. They're not being very discriminating in who they kill. Spending the night in a hotel, without telling anyone where you are, might be a smart move."

"You really think I'm in danger?"

"I don't know, but I think you should act as if you are. And if you're dead, I am short one key witness."

"I appreciate the beautiful sentiment."

I get off the phone and tell Richard I will need him to testify as well, especially about what happens tonight.

He nods his agreement. "Do you know what is really going on there?"

"I think I do. I read some of Heyer's papers. He saw a future where nuclear reactors would not be only these huge plants we know of today, but much smaller. They would provide power for more concentrated areas, cities, small towns, even neighborhoods, depending on the size."

"Okay . . ."

"And he claimed that he knew how to build them. They would be relatively compact, but they could provide massive heat and pressure that would yield power."

"And the heat and pressure is why it had to be underground."

I nod. "Right. And it would also protect against inadvertent radioactive leaks."

"But what you're talking about is not illegal."

"Very true, and Heyer said that on the phone that night when I called, remember? He said it was not illegal; I didn't know what he meant."

"What did he mean?"

"Did you ever watch the old *Superman* shows? With George Reeves?"

"Maybe a few. What does that have to do with anything?"

"There was one in which he used his tremendous power

to crush and heat a piece of coal . . . doing in a minute what it took nature years to do."

Richard is starting to understand; I can see it in his face. "So this is about . . ."

I nod. "Diamonds. Huge, perfect diamonds."

t's hard to believe that this has only been one day; it feels like a month.

The things that can go wrong are too long to list, and any one of them can keep Chris Myers in jail for the rest of his life. So all I can do is stare at the stupid phone and hope that when it rings, it's good news.

It's only rung a few times today. Twice it was Richard and once it was Corey, and in all three cases they reported that things were moving along as planned.

McKenny, as I expected, was very willing to go along with the planned raid on Metuska tonight. He wasn't thrilled with the idea of keeping it secret, but he went along provided he could hold the press conference when the allotted time was up. There was no way he was going to let the Feds in on this operation.

I can't be sure that Heyer is still alive, but I believe he is, and I hope so on more than one level. He could have suffered the same fate as Everson, Swain, Richter, and Burgess, but I doubt it. The conspirators did not need those people; they very much need Heyer. Those people represented a danger; Heyer represents success and immense wealth.

The plan is for McKenny and his team to go in just before midnight. Metuska shuts down for the night long before then, but I don't want to take any chances. We want the element of surprise, and we want to avoid giving Fulton and his people any ability to react.

I spend the afternoon preparing for the court session; it will obviously be crucial, but I'm hampered because the results of tonight's raid will determine a lot of what I can accomplish.

By ten o'clock Laurie and I are in the den drinking wine and waiting. There is a definite chance that we will be hammered by the time we hear from Corey or Richard, so we try to go slowly. We turn on the television, but neither of us has any interest in watching.

At 12:17, Corey calls. "Like clockwork. McKenny and his people were terrific; total pros."

"And Heyer?"

"Scared out of his mind, but alive and well. You should see Fulton; crying like a baby and implicating everybody."

"So much for the high pastor. Is Richard there?"

"Right here."

Corey puts him on the phone. "New Jersey State cops are taking custody of Heyer now. Not sure who will ultimately have custody, but right now it doesn't matter."

"Are things the way I expected?"

"Still a lot to be unraveled, but at this point I would say you hit it on the head."

"Great. You okay?"

"Andy, I cannot remember ever having this much fun."

Harold Caruso and Richard Wallace, my two witnesses today, are both in court when I arrive.

I head to the defense table, where Eddie is already seated. I'm a little late arriving because I was in Judge McVay's chambers, giving her and Daniel Morrow an update on what has happened, and what will happen today.

Both were shocked, and maybe a bit skeptical, but they agreed to give me some leeway.

Chris is brought in and takes his seat, and that prompts Caruso to get up and come over to us.

He pats Chris on the shoulder, and Chris says, "Thanks for doing this, Harold."

"I just hope it helps."

"Terrible about Vic."

Caruso nods sadly. "Yeah, but I think there's a lot about Vic that we didn't know."

Caruso takes his seat as the judge comes in. He just has to get back up a few minutes later, when I call him to the witness stand.

"Mr. Caruso, you work for Everson, Manning, and Winkler, a law firm in New York City?"

"I do."

"And when Mr. Myers worked there, you worked along with him in representing certain clients?"

"Yes."

"And you were friends with Mr. Myers as well? Outside of work?"

"Yes, for a very long time. I still consider him my friend."

"Did the clients you represented together include some of the townspeople of Metuska, Pennsylvania?"

"Yes."

I ask Caruso to describe the situation there, and what the case involved, and he talks about eminent domain and the town trying to take the land and homes from many of its people. Fortunately, he doesn't use "lawyer-speak," and he summarizes it accurately in a reasonably short time.

"At some point, did Mr. Myers leave the case?"

"Yes."

"Was that because of his arrest and conviction for involuntary manslaughter?"

Caruso nods sadly. "I'm afraid that it was."

"How was the case resolved, at least as it concerns your firm's involvement?"

"In Metuska? Well, Alex Swain, who organized the group and collected the money for legal fees, disappeared, and—"

"This is the same Alex Swain who we have recently learned was murdered around that time. His was the real identity for the man Mr. Myers was convicted of killing?"

"Yes, apparently so. When he left town, willingly or otherwise, the people thought he abandoned them and embezzled their money. But it left them with no resources and much less willingness to keep up the fight. A lot of them took the money offered for their homes and land and left town."

"How did your firm come to take the case in the first place? I mean, being so far from Metuska."

"I am not positive, but I believe that Vic Everson, our managing partner, heard about their situation and offered our services."

"You and Mr. Myers had no involvement in making that offer?"

"No."

I look toward the gallery and see that Richard Wallace has left the room, just as I had asked him to do.

"And are you aware that Victor Everson was himself murdered the night before last?"

"Tragically, yes."

"Do you know Paul Donnelly Sr.?"

Caruso looks surprised by the question. "Only by reputation."

"And that reputation is of an organized crime figure?"

"Yes."

"Did you know his son, Paul Donnelly Jr.? He was shot and killed, and the reports were that the target was actually his father."

"I knew Paul quite well; we went to college together."

"Did you know that he was actually the target of that shooting, and not his father?"

Caruso reacts with some surprise and sits up a little straighter in the chair. "No. I don't know that at all."

"Are you aware that a raid took place last night in Metuska, and it brought down the entire operation that was going on there? An operation regarding diamonds that has resulted in numerous murders and the unjust arrest and incarceration of Mr. Myers?"

Now Caruso is alert and clearly worried. "No . . . what are you—"

"And are you aware that witnesses have already identified you as a ringleader of that operation?"

"Hey, you can't—This is a load of bull. I'm not answering any more of your questions."

"You don't have to, Mr. Caruso. There are others that can do that for us."

At that moment, right on schedule, the door to the back opens and Richard comes back in with Clifford Heyer. A third man is with them; it is probably Heyer's attorney, which is unwelcome.

But it doesn't matter. Caruso sees Heyer, and fear and defeat both register in Caruso's eyes and face.

He slumps slightly and seems to shrink on the stand. A small man becomes smaller.

He knows it's over.

orrow attempts to cross-examine Caruso, but gets nowhere.

A shaken Caruso simply says, "I am not going to answer any more questions without the benefit of counsel." Since neither Morrow nor I are inclined to serve as his counsel, that effectively ends the cross-examination.

Caruso stands slowly and walks out of the courtroom. As per my plan with Richard, detectives from Paterson PD are waiting to arrest him and take him into custody.

I call Richard Wallace to the stand, which brings a murmur from the gallery that is so loud it could be more accurately called a rumbling. Richard looks serious as he takes the stand; not a hint of a smile despite the gallery reaction.

Daniel Morrow betrays no surprise at all, mainly because I informed him in chambers what was going to happen.

"Mr. Wallace, what is your occupation?"

"I am the chief prosecutor for Passaic County."

"Is this the first time testifying for the defense in a criminal trial that your office was prosecuting?"

"First and I hope the last."

"Please describe how you became involved with this case."

"You called me and asked if I would be a witness to certain events, and if I would then testify to them truthfully. I said that I would."

"Did it take some persuading?"

"Considerable."

"What finally convinced you?"

"You said it would contribute toward a search for the truth, which is what all trials are about."

"What was the first event you witnessed?"

"A telephone conversation between you and Clifford Heyer. You initiated the call."

"Who is Mr. Heyer?"

"He is an eminent nuclear physicist and a professor at MIT."

"Is he in this courtroom now?"

"Yes."

I take Richard through that phone call and through everything he learned during this whole process, right up through last night's raid. It's a fairly complete rendition and includes things that I was not aware of, including the fact that a panicked Fulton fully implicated Caruso and Donnelly.

And most important, Richard reports that Fulton said Donnelly ordered the killing of Charlie Burgess.

Game, set, and match.

I can feel Chris next to me wanting to jump out of his seat. Eddie puts his hand on Chris's shoulder to calm him down.

Much of what Richard has said could successfully be objected to by Morrow as hearsay. But he doesn't, maybe because he also wants to search for the truth, or maybe because it's Richard on the stand.

I turn Richard over to Morrow for cross-examination. He stands solemnly, walks over toward Richard. "Hi, boss . . . how are you?"

"I'm a little uncomfortable, but fine."

Morrow nods. "No further questions."

Judge McVay says, "Well, this has been a memorable morning. Mr. Carpenter, I have a motion you have filed which we will discuss outside the presence of the jury."

She sends the jury out and, once they leave, says, "You have a copy of the motion, Mr. Morrow. It is a request from the defense that I issue a directed verdict of acquittal, sua sponte. Would you like to respond?"

Sua sponte means that the judge will do it on her own, but I am sure she would like the prosecution to concur. I'd be fine either way.

Morrow stands. "Your Honor, ordinarily I would be inclined to move for the dismissal of all charges against Mr. Myers. But because of the involvement with the defense of my direct boss, Mr. Wallace, it seems as if that could be perceived as a conflict of interest.

"Having said that, I do not see any way, based on the evidence as presented, that the jury could return a verdict of guilty beyond a reasonable doubt. So we would not lodge an objection to a directed verdict if that is what you are inclined to do."

Judge McVay nods. "Thank you, Mr. Morrow. I understand the delicacy of your position. It is the ruling of this court that the defense motion is granted, and the directed verdict of acquittal is so ordered. I will speak to the jury in the jury room.

"Mr. Myers, you are free to go. I am sorry you had to go through this."

She slams down the gavel and that's it . . . it's over.

Chris turns to me, stunned. "Did what I think just happened actually happen?"

"It did."

"Andy, you're a genius."

"Aww, shucks . . . enough about me."

"There's a lot I still don't understand."

"We can talk about it tomorrow night at the party."

"There's going to be a party?" Chris asks, still bewildered.

"There's always a party."

The massive explosion happened at 4:14 the next morning.

It was felt for more than a mile; Denise Holman even called to tell me that it knocked pictures off her walls. It completely destroyed the construction that had been completed, sending tons of earth and cement down into the shaft, permanently destroying the reactor that had been installed there.

Fortunately, the plutonium had not been placed in the reactor yet, so there was no danger of radiation escaping. The placement was scheduled to happen soon, though once the raid had taken place it was no longer a consideration.

Government inspectors and the FBI initially had two possible suspects. One was Heyer himself; it is conceivable that he planted a timed device, so as to destroy his kidnappers' hopes of capitalizing on his work.

More likely culprits were people whose wealth depends on the value of naturally formed diamonds. If that is the case, it is not known how they eluded guards surrounding the property to plant the explosives, though it is quite possible that money changed hands.

That will all be the subject of further investigation.

If history is our guide, progress cannot be stopped. Ultimately someone as smart as Heyer will resurrect this type of project. Then perhaps people will no longer pay obscene amounts of money for little stones that do nothing other than look pretty.

Our victory parties have two main requirements. One, they almost always take place at Charlie's Sports Bar. And two, we only have them when we win.

Victory parties after a loss tend toward the depressing.

We always take the private upstairs room. It doesn't have quite as much of the sports bar feel, but the burgers and beer are the same, which is damn good.

Here tonight are Chris Myers, Corey, Marcus, Sam, Eddie, Richard Wallace, Willie, Sondra, Vince, and Pete. Willie and Sondra weren't a part of the case, but because they know Chris so well and took care of Killian and her puppies, they belong.

Vince and Pete had absolutely nothing to do with anything, and they weren't invited, but they have internal "free-food sensors," which led them here. And they're welcome.

Actually, Willie dropped Sondra off and left to run an errand. He said he'd be back soon.

I promised Chris I would try to explain whatever he didn't know. It doesn't take him long before he gets me to sit with him and do just that.

"So how did you know it was Caruso?" is his first question.

"That was actually one of the last things I realized. But it all followed from realizing that it was about making the fake diamonds. Not that they're really fake."

"Then what made you know it was about diamonds?"

"A couple of things. For one, Fulton had a phone conversation with a diamond broker who is involved with securing and placing expensive gems. That's what Paul Donnelly Jr. did as well, so I looked at it through the prism of him being the target at the restaurant, not his father. Maybe the shooter didn't miss after all.

"When I spoke to Heyer and mentioned Donnelly, he said it was a shame about him. I didn't know what he meant because I thought he was talking about the father. But he wasn't, and I realized that later. He was talking about the son getting shot and killed.

"Then it all fit. Heyer had written about the pressure and heat his reactor could generate, and I knew from *Superman* that that is how perfect diamonds are formed."

"*Superman?*"

"It's a long story. But the key thing is that Heyer said what they were doing was not illegal, and it wasn't. There's no law against creating man-made diamonds; it's done all the time. But they are all small stones, and it's generally detectable.

"Heyer would have been able to make big stones . . . incredibly valuable. There are types of diamonds that sell for over a million dollars a carat."

Corey has overheard us, and he comes over. "But if it was legal, why murder to protect it?"

"Because it had to remain a secret. They could get their stones into the marketplace at huge prices. But if it became known that diamonds could be produced at will, all kinds of all sizes and grades, then the market would go through the floor. It wouldn't be special anymore.

"The other reason was that there are powerful interests out there who make huge fortunes from diamonds. They finance wars with them . . . blood diamonds. They would not just accept this. They killed Paul Jr., and I'll bet they were responsible for that explosion in Metuska this morning."

"But how did you know it was Caruso?"

"A few things. For one, he was part of a group of friends with you, Jessica, and Paul Jr. So if Paul Jr. was the target of that shooting, that would mean he was going to be the one to pass the jewels. Therefore Caruso became a suspect.

"More importantly, Caruso had told me that Swain had called him and told him he sold his house and was bailing out on the town. I had forgotten that for a while. Once Swain turned up dead, it became obvious that that conversation could not have happened.

"Plus, Caruso told me he was at the Basement Bar with you the night Swain was killed, but he left early. He was just making sure everything was arranged perfectly."

Chris nods. "And they set me up because I was going to bring in the state. Once I talked to Fornes, my fate was sealed."

"Right. So the three players were eliminated. They killed Swain, they set you up, and they faked a harassment thing against Fornes. There will be an investigation now; he'll get rehired, and his boss will go down if he was in on it, which he probably was.

"The lucky break was that it took Heyer a long time to

build the machine. Otherwise they would have been off and running."

"And the Fellows? Is that a real religion?" Corey asks.

I shake my head. "No, I'm sure it was just a cover. It gave them privacy and a way to shield their money. That's why they never tried to recruit anyone. Instead they wanted to clear out the town so they could operate freely, with no government to get in their way or snoop around."

"So they kidnapped Swain and killed him behind the bar or brought him there already dead?" Chris asks.

"I'm not sure. But they probably held him for a couple of days and then killed him that night, either behind the bar or nearby. It didn't matter once they paid off Burgess and the bartender. I was told the bartender was already arrested for perjury."

"So Paul Jr. was part of this? I never would have thought so."

I nod. "He had to be. Keep in mind, making these stones was not illegal. He might not have known about the rest of it, but I can't say for sure. It's possible he saw this as a way of getting into business with Daddy without becoming a criminal. We'll never know all of it; Daddy is going away for the rest of his life."

"I can't believe you pulled this off," Chris says.

"I had no choice. We need you at the Foundation. You're a dog lover; you should get one of your own."

The door opens, and I say, "Or two of your own."

Willie walks in with Killian on a leash, and carrying one of her puppies. He comes over to Chris, puts the puppy in his lap, and hands him Killian's leash.

"I can have them both? Mother and child?"

I smile. "I can't think of a better home for them. Merry Christmas."

"Thanks, but it's not Christmas anymore."

I look over at Laurie. "That depends on who you talk to."